The Sons of Light

'David Rudkin is an odd man out amongst modern British dramatists. His plays (like *Afore Night Come, Ashes* or *Cries from Casement*) are a unique blend of ritual and realism, of Artaudian imagery and bloodshot language. They are filled with metaphors of blindness, anal violation and excretion, yet they also show a preoccupation with biblical and classical fable.'

Guardian

First staged in Newcastle and subsequently by the Royal Shakespeare Company in both Stratford and London, *The Sons of Light* is '180 minutes of compelling theatre and a feat of such tremendous imagination that it makes most other current fringe productions look like the scraping from David Rudkin's fingernails'.

Evening Standard

'Set in one of the remotest Scottish islands, the play exhibits two kinds of repression; an unseen landowner keeps the islanders in spiritual darkness while sanctioning an underworld complex in which enslavement is, in the name of science, given horrifically exact embodiment. To the island come a new pastor and his three sons, who finally succeed in liberating both strata — and, incidentally, in freeing an island girl from possession, otherwise called schizophrenia.'

Observer

'. . . a work of reckless imagination, a daredevil leap into the outer reaches of the dramatically unfashionable and unruly . . . but undeniably refreshing in the context of an English stage usually so stingy with its imagination and skimpy in its invention.'

New Statesman

'Mr Rudkin's conception has the simplicity of myth and the ingenious naivety of science fiction. Like his first play *Afore Night Come, The Sons of Light* is a savage moral fable.'

Sunday Times

The front cover shows a scene from the Tyneside Theatre Company production in 1978. Photo . . . The photograph of David Rudkin . . . on the . . . courtesy of the Birmingham . . . Repertory . . .

David Rudkin

THE SONS OF LIGHT

EYRE METHUEN · LONDON

First published in 1981 by Eyre Methuen Ltd,
11 New Fetter Lane, London EC4P 4EE.
Copyright © 1981 by David Rudkin
ISBN 0 413 49120 X

Printed in Great Britain by
Fakenham Press Limited, Fakenham, Norfolk
Set in IBM 10pt Journal by 𝟕\ Tek-Art, Croydon, Surrey

Characters

In order of appearance:

BENGRY, *a Pastor*
SAMUEL
MICHAEL   *his twin sons*
JOHN, *his eldest son*

NEAND, *Chief Elder*
YAGG, *Deacon*
ELDER YESCANAB
CHILD MANATOND
MANATOND, *Elder*
SISTER DUINHEAD, *Deaconess*
SISTER CROY
YESCANAB, *Elder Yescanab's son*

Scarweth, *previous Pastor*
HOLST
Guards
Miss WEMWOOD
Doctor NEBEWOHL
An Escapee
GOWER
BLACKIE
Chuck
A Boy-Woman, *demented and deformed*
A Girl-Man, *demented and deformed*
Soldiers

Roles given here in lower-case letters can be doubled by members of the Company — who at minimum should number four women and thirteen men.

The action of the play takes place at the present time, on a volcanic island far out in the Atlantic from the north-west coast of Europe.

In its original form (1965-66; working-title *The Sea*) THE SONS OF LIGHT would have played some eight or nine hours. Several reworkings were attempted: in 1967; 1969-71; and in 1975 an entire restructuring, again very long. From this and the original version, a performing text was extracted for the play's first production, March 1976, by the Tyneside Theatre Company at the University Theatre, Newcastle; where it played for just under three hours, with the following cast:

BENGRY	Leonard Maguire
SAMUEL	Ron Cook
MICHAEL	Chris Tainton
JOHN	Ian Hogg
NEAND	David Steuart
YAGG	Sean Scanlan
ELDER YESCANAB	Andrew Crawford
CHILD MANATOND	Jennie Stoller
ELDER MANATOND	Fred Pearson
SISTER DUINHEAD	Arwen Holm
SISTER CROY	Pam Wingfield
YESCANAB	Alun Armstrong
HOLST	Cornelius Garrett
NEBEWOHL	Harold Innocent
DAME EVELYN WEM	Patricia England
GOWER	Jonathan Kent
BLACKIE	Tom Nicholls
Designer	Maria Bjørnson
Director	Keith Hack

BENGRY, NEAND, ELDER YESCANAB, SAMUEL and MICHAEL doubled as SOLDIERS in Act IV; YAGG doubled as CHUCK and as a GUARD; ELDER MANATOND doubled as a GUARD; HOLST doubled as SCARWETH, as an islander CROY, and as an officer with NEBEWOHL, CAPTAIN WASTWOOD. GOWER played also the ESCAPEE in Act II (a doubling that is also psychologically valid) and a SOLDIER in Act IV (a doubling that is theatrically perilous). BLACKIE played also an ISLANDER and a GUARD. For the Demented and Deformed (who appeared with Scarweth in Act II) children were cast from local schools.

For the Stratford production, November 1977, by the Royal Shakespeare Company at The Other Place, further revisions, cuts and rewrites were done, toward this final version printed here. Again the playing time, without intervals, was just under three hours.

BENGRY	Edwin Richfield
SAMUEL	Ron Cook
MICHAEL	Anton Lesser
JOHN	Nigel Terry
NEAND	Morris Perry
YAGG	Ian McNeice
ELDER YESCANAB	Roy Purcell
CHILD MANATOND	Charlotte Cornwell
ELDER MANATOND	John Rhys-Davies
SISTER DUINHEAD	Anne Raitt
SISTER CROY	Roberta Taylor
YESCANAB	Peter McEnery
HOLST	Dominic Jephcott
MISS WEMWOOD	Sheila Allen
NEBEWOHL	Alan David
GOWER	Simon Rouse
BLACKIE	Jack Klaff
Designer	Ralph Koltai
Director	Ron Daniels
Sound	Leo Leibovici, David Rudkin

Here MICHAEL and SAMUEL doubled as SOLDIERS in Act IV; NEAND as SCARWETH; YAGG as CHUCK and as a GUARD; BLACKIE as a GUARD and the BOY DEMENTED AND DEFORMED: SISTER CROY as the GIRL DEMENTED AND DEFORMED. The characters of CAPTAIN WASTWOOD and DAME EVELYN WEM were conflated and reconceived, becoming the altogether new MISS WEMWOOD. GOWER doubled as the ESCAPEE in Act II and a SOLDIER in Act IV.

Author's Note

Bengry's Welshness is in his verbal patterns rather than in any 'accent'; the Walian tune should be minimal. John's Ulster (as the text suggests) is somewhat stronger, though nothing so strong as the twins'. The islanders' speech is a fusion of Gaelic and Nordic elements, its base Orkney rather than Hebridean: the dialect is my own invention, its archaisms a metaphor of the islanders' regression (it will be noticed how Yescanab and Child Manatond begin to transcend this). Nebewohl's Teutonicism is again rather in his syntax than in any Tcherman eccent. Miss Wemwood is neither cold nor monstrous, but a soul simply and totally committed to her own chosen technology of salvation, as is any ideologue; as is Bengry, indeed; or John, come to that. The role of Gower is peculiarly difficult: a temptation any player must resist is to *illustrate* his inner condition to an audience, but this must a Gower most of all resist — rather, through that ease and simplicity with which he experiences his own self, seduce the audience into his own ruined head. If not, the entire relationship with Yescanab is rendered meaningless.

The soundtrack is more a cinematic than a theatrical one. For all that, it is always allusive, never literal: my specifications for it are integral to the text, and to be respected as such. The Company will need a process-period of at least six weeks. At production-weekend, the Director would be wise to allow for a two-day technical on sound-cues alone.

The Newcastle production, on a large proscenium stage, had a monumental, operatic, hallucinatory visual presence. At the Other Place, as befits a limited 'empty space' with audience on three sides, the staging was sparer, and the experience of the play more morally internal. Both productions were rigorous in their search for truth, and either form of staging is perfectly viable.

In both productions, for the fog scenes, smoke was used.

From its beginning, the play was dedicated to

Doctor Robert Ollendorff
himself a resurrectioner

Ollendorff was a Reichian therapist whose patient and disciple I had been, and of whom Nebewohl is a portrait-in-reverse. Ollendorff died before the play was ever performed; but the dedication stands.

D.R.

Part One

The Division
of the Kingdom

Act One

Desolation: rock, ocean, bogland. Wind, spare curlew-cry. Enter
PASTER BENGRY *bearing boy* SAMUEL *across his arms.*

BENGRY. Lie you here now. Samuel. Son. Shadow of this peat.
A while. Till we are met . . . No thicket here to hide no ram.
Rock, peat, hagg. (*Gaunt humour:*) Shiver? Shall warm you.
Best nor any gift *I'll* have, to warm you.

SAMUEL (*bleak*). Why are we not met? Could be it's not the
time for our coming, Father. Too late, an' the brethren
anghery. Or a time too soon, them not prepared.

BENGRY. Foolish virgins? One evening the week only, autumn,
that little plane flies out across this deep. The brethren know
that we are here. Michael? John? *As they arrive, poor,
burdened with scraps of luggage.*

MICHAEL. Da?

JOHN. Father?

BENGRY. Sit. Till we are met. Consider your new dwellingplace.
John. Sit.

JOHN. How are ye, Sam?

SAMUEL. Your voices sounds close. Yet tiny an' far away.

MICHAEL. Dee-lirrium.

JOHN. The flight, and our descent.

SAMUEL. Don't want to go on no plane no more —

JOHN. This island's reached only by plane, Sam. No ships: across
that deep: except to take the quarrystone away.

SAMUEL. I'll go by water when I go.

MICHAEL. Thon mountain, John.

JOHN. Volcanic. Dead.

MICHAEL (*suddenly*). Here's men, Da.

NEAND, YAGG, ELDER YESCANAB *are slowly come.*

NEAND (*arriving*). Pastor? Pastor Bengry? *Accent of a remote
Scottish island quality but with strong Nordic element.*

BENGRY (*warm*). Brother!

NEAND. (*A deep Christian inner stillness, gentle but stark*). Jacob Neand: Chief Elder. Welcome, Pastor, in the Name of the Lord, to our island of Out Skaranay.

ELDERS (*a murmur*). Aymen, aymen . . .

BENGRY (*warm*). Brother Neand . . .

NEAND (*gentle, inflexible*). Chief Elder.

BENGRY. Such loving service, I hear you have rendered your community, this tragic interval: since my poor predecessor . . . (*Uneasy pause.*)

NEAND. Adam Yagg. Deacon and colleague at our island schuil . . .

YAGG. Pastor . . .

NEAND. Andrew Yescanab. Elder. Keeper of our shop.

BENGRY (*warm, shaking their hands*). Brethren in the Blood of Jesus —

NEAND. So. These yuir sons. Shall so luik forward, Pastor Bengry, to the teaching of yuir sons. Brainy, we hear. Eh, Deacon Yagg?

YAGG (*young, uncomplicated-sounding*). Ay Pastor . . .

BENGRY (*gentle*). No, brother Neand, brother Yagg. My Michael and Samuel shall not be going to your school, I'm sorry . . .

NEAND. Such lanterns of learning at our desks, great privilege . . .

BENGRY. I made this plain.

NEAND (*unhearing*). Great privilege.

SAMUEL. Father is our teacher, Sir.

MICHAEL. And John.

SAMUEL. John is our mother too. Since our earthly mother died.

MICHAEL. We know Greek!

SAMUEL. Botany as well.

NEAND (*charmed: ruffling their heads*). Ah, but shall all be different now. Heh? This is not Ireland. Here all guid boys must come to schuil.

A movement of them away: except:

MICHAEL. Sammy what's thon? (*A subhuman shape there, no-one has noticed till now.*) In the name o' God, Sammy, whatever's thon? Is it woman or mahn?

SAMUEL. Can't tell.

MICHAEL. Go up you till it Sammy. See if it has breasts. Or a beard on its face . . .

SAMUEL (*no nearer*). Is weemen has beards. Like thon at Limavady Fair. One breast an' half a beard. Hermaffeydite. You go.

MICHAEL. You go. Came intil the world an hour ahead of me, you go.

SAMUEL. Came intil this world an hour ahind of me, you do what I say: go you.

MICHAEL. Not movin' any. Could be it's daid. Da a funerell his first day. (*Tentative whisper:*) Hi . . .

SAMUEL. Hi . . .

MICHAEL. You there.

SAMUEL. You.

No response.

MICHAEL. Anyone at home? I'll huff an' I'll puff an' I'll blow yuir house down. Ff, ff . . .

SAMUEL (*whispers in its other ear*). He's Micha El.

MICHAEL. He's Samu El.

SAMUEL. We're the Pastor's sons. What name are you?

No response.

MICHAEL. Dumb?

SAMUEL. Deaf. (*A tentative crack of thumbs.*)

MICHAEL. Blind?

SAMUEL. Not breathin' any. Look but. A tear. It *is* alive.

MICHAEL. A woman then.

SAMUEL. Men cry.

They peer up into its face.

JOHN (*returned beyond*). You two. (*Brings them and luggage away.*)

MICHAEL. A poor creature, John . . .

SAMUEL. A lump of flesh . . .

They go.

THIS THING. Whui is these like stars appearen'? Shaik-Et, Maik-Et ahn' Tui-Baid-Ye-Go . . . Intil mine fiery furness: tss, tss . . . (*Rails after with a mad crowing.*) The Cock o' God a-wooin' go! Spit milk, spit milk! (*Then, childlike, mimics small aircraft landing from above.*) Great white machanacal baird. Eiggs shallnae hatch. Heir's stony ground. (*Scrambles off after.*)

People gathering.

ELDER YESCANAB (*somewhat breathless from having climbed; quiet, justly proud*). Well Pastor. Yuir house.

BENGRY. High enough. Brother Yescanab. To be a beacon, eh? Proud little settlement too, Brother: that we came through. Been some rebuilding?

ELDER YESCANAB. All that was old, was all grubbed up; built up, new. By our great Benefactor. Bless his name.

OTHER ELDERS. Aymen . . . Lord bless his name . . .

NEAND. And a fine new schoolhouse. Sir Wendell Bain has built us. Pastor. As yuir boys shall see. Oh . . . He has been a great great giver, Sir Wendell Bain. A great — *giver* . . .

BENGRY. And the chapel his rebuilding too?

YAGG. Our glory and our pride.

BENGRY. Striking sight, that. White chapel, out on that black headland.

NEAND. Pastor. (*Bringing him to a man in a wheelchair.*) Elder Manatond. (*Seems richly proud in him.*)

MANATOND (*In mid-prime, slumped, mortal, head-heavy, aged before his time*). A wuid stahnd, sor. But ye see A've nae but the mockeries o' leigs.

BENGRY (*moved*). Yet you make your way up this rough high place to welcome me. Brother. (*Warm handshake.*) And is this a son of yours, has wheeled you Brother? What is his — ?

NEAND. Elder Manatond is our mason, Pastor. In his stoneyard all our crosses be made.

MANATOND. Well Pastor, A'm fit to no more now than watch this lad here labour at the stone in mine behalf . . .

BENGRY. This young man —

NEAND. Pastor. Our Deaconess. Sister Duinhead. (*Bringing him to a young woman of blazing chaste radiance.*)

BENGRY. A Deaconess . . .

SISTER DUINHEAD. Pastor . . .

BENGRY. . . . so young?

SISTER DUINHEAD. Pastor. Welcome in the Love of the Redeemer.

BENGRY (*offering a very warm handshake*). Sister . . .

NEAND. Pastor. A member of our sisterhuid. Sister Croy.

SISTER CROY (*She has bread and fish, a gift for him*). Welcome among us, Pastor.

BENGRY (*impressed*). Thank you, Sister Croy. — And this lad? What office does he hold?

ELDER YESCANAB. None Sir. An helper. Guid Elder Manatond has tuik him till his side. Apprentice. In his stoneyard, now he himself is paralised. . . . Mine sone, Sir. An helper . . .

BENGRY (*gently*). What is your name? Look at me.

NEAND. He's —

BENGRY. Your name, tell me yourself —

MANATOND. The Pastor yuir name, lad. He willnae eit your heid.

LAD (*own name tangling in throat*). Y— Ye— Sc— Nab . . . Sir.

MANATOND. 'Yescanab, Yescanab': the name yuir mother an' yuir father gave ye.

YESCANAB (*at last*). S— T— Phn. S—stephen sir.

BENGRY. Stephen? No name to be ashamed of. Michael, tell him, who was Stephen?

MICHAEL. First Christian martyr, Da. Put to death with cruel stones.

SAMUEL. Stèphanos is the Greek for a crown.

MANATOND. Oh, Head Master, here's an pair of pupils. And of an age to confound us elders in the tample, eh? Oh Pastor Bengry, King ye shuid be called.

BENGRY. Why, Brother?

MANATOND. To have got such princely sons.

NEAND (*sotto*). Puir Elder Manatond . . . But the child that he himself was blest with . . . If blest we can say . . .

YAGG. If child we can call it.

BENGRY. It, Brother Yagg? (*Sees whom they mean, the subhuman thing lurking at a distance.*)

ELDER YESCANAB. The house is ready, Pastor. Food's there, to tide ye; the lamps are filled.

BENGRY. Thank you, Brother. Such news is always good. John. Mick. Sam. In. (*They go.*) Stout stone, Brother Yagg. Tough buildin'. The good Sir Wendell's work, heh?

ELDERS (*obscure murmur*). Ay . . . Lord bless his name . . .

SISTER DUINHEAD. Hallelujah! Lord bless Sir Wendell's name!

YAGG. We speak of the man to whuim we owe our survival here. Who brought us work and purpose.

ISLANDERS. Aymen, aymen.

NEAND. Well, Pastor? An prayer? To bless yuir coming here?

OTHERS (*fervent, glad*). Ay Pastor!

BENGRY (*at last, simply*). Let there be light.

Surprised by the brevity, at last they go.

Inrolling wavecrash: backwash carded by clattering pebbles. Cold bright morning. Chapel bell's call to worship midfar. MICHAEL, SAMUEL playing: fragments of flotsam used for comical dress.

SAMUEL. This is a stormbeach. The deep's hurled in huge terraces of stones. (*Pause.*) There's That again.

This lump of flesh, CHILD MANATOND, heaves itself into sluggish life.

Don't run away. We're only the Pastor's sons.

MICHAEL. He's Samu El.

SAMUEL. He's Micha El. What name are you?

MICHAEL. Tell us your name, we told ye ours.

SAMUEL. Tell us your name.

CHILD MANATOND (*convulsive noises form dark, slow, ugly in throat: become a voice, black, void*). N— . . . N— . . . Nun.

SAMUEL. A holy sister.

CHILD MANATOND. N— . . . N— . . . Not . . .

MICHAEL. If yui're a knot, then let's untie ye.

Twins giggle at own humour.

CHILD MANATOND. N— N— Nobody.

Pause.

MICHAEL. It says its name is Nobody.

SAMUEL. This is not nobody. If this is nobody, then I poke nobody's eye. And I rend nobody's gorgonsnaky locks.

CHILD MANATOND *begins to heave, childishly tittering.*

An' I kick nobody, an' nobody feels pain!

CHILD MANATOND (*shrieks, laughs, a mandrake unearthed. Suddenly through its mouth a new voice: mother-persona, barren, destructive*). Sheela. Sheela! (*A third voice answers: child-persona, weak, unformed.*) Maa . . . ? (*Mother.*) Come away Sheela. Nasty mein. Ahind ma this minute, Sheela. Down! (*Child.*) Maa . . . ? (*Mother.*) Guid. No child heir.

SAMUEL. It *is* a woman.

CHILD MANATOND (*fourth voice: father-persona, repugnant, devouring*). Mahn. Mahn. Eh? Sebastian? Son? (*Child.*) Daa . . . ? (*Father.*) Mahn-son. Mahnson. (*Child.*) Daa . . . ?

MICHAEL. Mahn as well?

SAMUEL. Make up yuir mind.

MICHAEL (*to* JOHN *approaching*). Here's an uncertain person, John. All voices mixed in the one poor head.

SAMUEL. Like him who said 'My name is Legion for I is many.' Five or six souls, in the one poor shell of mortal clay.

JOHN. Well that'll take some sortin' out in the Resurrection, won't it?

SAMUEL. This is our brother, John —

SISTER DUINHEAD (*screaming in like a bird*). No . . ! No . . !

MICHAEL. Whui's this when she's at home?

SISTER DUINHEAD (*racked on a rage that curls vortiginously up within her*). Yuis are to leave this poor creature its lone! D'yuis heir? Stand away from it. Far. Far. (*Relaxes, crooning, trembling.*) Oh . . . Poor child. Puir flame of God, mine love, mine love . . .

MICHAEL (*impressed*). Are you its mother?

SISTER DUINHEAD. Its mother of this earth is dead.

SAMUEL. Its sister then?

SISTER DUINHEAD. Its sister in Christ. (*A terrifying fulfilledness. Then:*) Nor any road is this, His Sabbath, to be dreissed. Coloury, wild an' Babalonish dreissed. Twins of ye, an mockery of lad uir lass. 'Male and female created He them'! An' yui, John Bengry Pastorson their aildest, shuid know better. Wheir's yuir black?

ELDERS *meanwhile gathered.*

BENGRY (*quietly arrived*). Yes Michael. Samuel, John. Dress for chapel. God's Day Gloom's Day. Dress in black.

Sons going, suddenly MICHAEL *jukes mischievously back.*

MICHAEL. Hi. Sister Duinhead. (*He offers four fingers, two of each hand, crossed in a square.*) Put your finger in the crow's nest.

SAMUEL (*penitent*). Ay Sister Duinhead. Put yui yuir finger in the crow's nest.

MICHAEL. Put yui yuir finger in the crow's nest. The crow's not at home.

SISTER DUINHEAD *scents some trap, but yet must be the better of her worst suspicions. Suffering the children, she allows* SAMUEL *to nod her finger toward the nest of* MICHAEL'S *fingers crossed luring her there. She dips her finger: dip, dip . . . Nothing happens untoward.*

MICHAEL. *The crow's away*
    to Ballybay
    to pluck a white stone . . .

SISTER DUINHEAD *condescending dips her finger deeply in —*

MICHAEL (*suddenly*). *The crow's home, the crow's home!*

Fingers clamped round hers like a vice, SISTER DUINHEAD *screams, can hardly haul free.*

CHILD MANATOND. Ha ha ha ha! Micha El! Ha ha ha ha!

Twins scamper clamorous away.

MICHAEL. Duinhead Dunghead!

Gone. BENGRY *shows nothing.*

SISTER DUINHEAD. The Sabbath is not mocked.

BENGRY (*new hint of a grim purposive hardness*). No, radiant sister. Nor any of the week.

SISTER DUINHEAD. Has given us His Sign.

ELDERS ETC (*stricken*). Aymen.

NEAND. Ay Pastor: cruel Sign . . .

SISTER DUINHEAD. Cruel, Elder Neand? A Sign for great rejoicing and great joy! (*Vivid, simple, with minimal drama.*) Nine yeirs ago; an autumn Sabbath, very much the light an' like of this; twenty of us, childer-that-was, on our way to yuir predecessor's Sabbath class, was met by — an mahn we'd trusted — how not? Our Deacon of that time —

NEAND. Devil, devil . . .

SISTER DUINHEAD. Which Deacon stuid. Waylayed us by an gait; strange eye in his heid. 'Stop'. An greit box he had, shut, fornent him on the ground. 'Luik'. Opened it. 'See'. Garments, ha tuik out: coloury, rough; wild. 'For childern to weir,' sayed he. 'Och sir, wa musna linger. Sabbath, sir . . .' Crowns, ha tuik out. Baubles. Strings o' shells. 'Is these not pretty?' 'Sabbath, sir . . . Sabbath . . .' 'An Sabbath play, thein. Nebuchadnezzar. Or Daniel — ay, Daniel, in the Den. Whui'll play the lions' parts?' 'Me. Me,' we some of us sayed. 'Hush thein. A secret. Secret play. With me . . .'

An strand. Along the Sound. 'Here's Babalon,' sayed he; 'get dreissed.' 'But sir — ' 'An Sabbath play, an Babalon play. Put on ye.' . . . 'Which lahds'll play the weemen, ha?' Skirts ha brought out; for the lahds to weir. 'Ahn whui'll play wicked parts?' 'Me! Me!' Sticks ha gave us, coloury, soft, to paint ourselves. We painted an' we dressed.

'Nebuchadnezzar King o' the Jews, Sold his wife for a pair o' shoes!' We laughed. 'Heir is an candle to light her to beid. Chop off her heid!' We laughed. 'Daniel's in the Lions' Den! Be lions! Bite at him!' We bit at him. We laughed. 'Three boys nbw, to be thrusted in the royal stoves!' 'Me! Me! Me!' 'Shadrach, Meshech and Abed-Nego!' 'Me! Me! Me!' 'Be fire: an' burn at them!' Ssss. Ssss. We played these things.

I grew afeared. I hid. I crept. I ran. Tui ma house: 'Ma, Da . . .' We ran: 'Brother, Sister. Elder . . .' The town ran: 'Pastor . . . Pastor Scarweth!'

Strand. Empty. Own clothes sheid, all childer gone. From the water an trumpet-note. Voice. Him. Scarweth's Deacon. 'See heir, yuis Sabbath-fearin' fools, yuir childer ride wi' me God's deep on this His so-called Day!' An boat: move out: toward the open Sound: all childer aboard, wild, coloury, Babalonish-dreissed, faces painted; masks, crowns; sexes crossed; an garish ride upon the deep . . . And his voice, rail: 'Luik down then, Lord, on us defile Yuir 'Day'. An taste o' Yuir Wrath, ha? Show us!'

Laughter. Screams. We run, clamber, scramble: clifftop, shore. Some of us reach the wall of Sir Wendell's demesne, was buildin' thein. Himself is with us; stands with us; watches; sees; hears. The screams. Faint. Fainter. Silent. Boat, small, smaller on the deep. Toward Black Head. Beyonder. Toward Cape Yell; and the north wild water.

Two days an' nights, the boat we see again. Upturned shell. Day by day after, that sea bring in its grim receipts. Green shirt, Sheila-MacNair's-that-was. Yelley ribbon, Willie Scairth had in his hair. Lion-mask, crown. An scarlet frock, Andhrew Croy had wore . . . All innocent childrehuid, warm live laughter, childerflesh, led on to stray, in green an' yelley an' reid, to be swallowed up in that grey deep. Thus. Out of that clear cold sky, His — Furyhammer fell. Bolt glorious, pitying nuir beauty nuir no youthfulness. Only I, through mine guid dread, spared. (*Chapel bell has ceased.*) And paid his price. Pastor, so-called, Scarweth. Haunted ever after by the sound o' theim, the nineteen that his negligence had drowned: the cries o' them he wuid heir, he sayed, cry 'Help us Help us' from the deep. Which voices brought him, in his end, till his mad deith; to walk out after theim, to follow theim an' join theim, in that deep himself.

And now we heir, how ye intend ta intherduce among us . . . an strange observance . . .

ELDERS (*relieved that this subject at last is broached; but uneasy*). Ay Pastor . . .

SISTER DUINHEAD. How we are all, from now, to take, at the Breakin' of Breid, the Blood of Jesus, from one common chalice . . .

BENGRY. A symbol: how we must be one together in His Redeeming. From now, one Chalice. Yes. One Steward: to stand at the Table of the Lord. All to approach; kneel there; and take, from him. It is a truer ceremony.

NEAND. I do not like to think how Sir Wendell Bain shall take to this.

BENGRY. What should so disquiet him? The Blood of Life gathered in one Vessel?

YAGG. You turn our ceremony upside down.

ELDER YESCANAB (*uneasy*). Pastor. Ye say one steward only. Which wuid this one steward be?

BENGRY (*considers their unease*). Yes. (*At last.*) Stephen —

NEAND (*almost inaudible*). Pastor . . .

BENGRY. Look at me. Hold up your head — What fear of touch is this? Hands do not burn; nor eyes do not. Look in my eyes. (*Has* YESCANAB *at last do so.*) The well is deep. (*Has him hold his gaze.*) What other well was said to be deep?

YESCANAB. J — Jacob's Well — Pastor —

BENGRY. Whom had Our Redeemer met, by this well?

YESCANAB. The W-oman of Samaria. Pastor . . .

BENGRY. (*Considers him. Then:*) Here is my steward.

YESCANAB. No. No Pastor —

SISTER CROY. Pastor, he's the last —

BENGRY (*bleak logic*). Where shall that 'last' be placed though, when the many are called, the few are chosen? Stephen —

ELDER YESCANAB. Pastor, A beig ye —

NEAND. Pastor, the lad's — not fit — I taught him, Pastor —

YAGG. We taught him, and we know.

BENGRY. Taught him, and he is not fit?

NEAND (*closer*). Pastor, the lad's forever strayin' in some — furnace in the head.

BENGRY. I can see that. Brother Manatond?

MANATOND (*strangely exhausted*). I say nothing. If you say.

BENGRY. Thank you, Brother. Stephen. At the chapel you'll find Michael and Samuel: they'll tell you the order of service and instruct you what to do. Go on.

YESCANAB (*at last*). Pastor.

A silence for him going.

YAGG (*sotto*). This Pastor makes a mock of us.

SISTER DUINHEAD (*sotto*). Courage, Deacon. It shall pass.

BENGRY. To the chapel. All of you. All of you! Must I stone you there?

NEAND (*brings others quietly away*). As before Rimmon, we shall bow for now . . .

SISTER DUINHEAD. Our God is in our hearts.

ELDER YESCANAB. Sir Wendell shall put all right again.

Goes.

CHILD MANATOND. Ha ha! Punch an' Judy rode till chapel thron-ed on an rotted apple —

SISTER DUINHEAD (*to bring away with her*). Child Manatond
. . .

CHILD MANATOND. *The rotted apple broke in twui:*
wha' shall Punch an' Judy dui?

BENGRY. Child?

CHILD MANATOND (*mother, childish, black*): No child heir.

BENGRY. Child Manatond. Wheel your father.

Inside the chapel: gloom, a Cross; YESCANAB *with chalice.*

YESCANAB. They hate me, at this Table o' the Lord. All their hatred of the change, tha visit on mine heid. Strange, but: A enjoy that . . . 'Take. Drink.' Fuil, Bengry: pronounce mine well is deep: am A such glass, ye see mine secret Sodom heart? Make me his ministrant! Trust Christ's Blood . . . When what Chalice A dreims for, of an night, is of a . . . husband . . . enter me . . . Ram, cleave mine afters open: stretch . . . See that, Welsh Bengry? In mine 'deep well'? Oh Stephen, handmaid of the Lord indeed. That A am wrongshapen as an mahn . . . Oh . . . An holy image now A see all right. Maself: on mine back, lie, eyes ti' Heaven, mine afters up, up over above ma very face, arse of me, an table spreid baneath God's sky, an anvil for his Gannet's dive — ah, oh . . . See that? Bengry sees nought. Nought to see. Mine body is mine grave. This island . . .

A high place. A raven-croak wheels in, away. Muted quarry-sounds.
MICHAEL *arrived;* BENGRY, SAMUEL. JOHN *following.*

MICHAEL (*declaiming*). Mine are the highest eyes on the island! From high Ben Gabriel I see all!

BENGRY. What do you see, Michael?

MICHAEL. A wall, Da. Divide the island, west till east. Quarry . . . A harbour there. Ship, look. Castle . . . North toward Cape Yell there. What need Sir Wendell wall half the island till himself? Sojers.

JOHN. What?

MICHAEL. Sojers. The length of his fortress roof there, all rigid till attention. Luik.

JOHN. You have sharp sight . . . Chimneys, surely.

MICHAEL. Sojers. Ahoy! A'hoy'i'hoy'i'ho! Black sojermen, stand to! Stand to, the guard! (*Mock stenfire.*) Ba'a'a'a'a'a'a 'a'a'a'A! (*Sudden little gasp. Recovering.*) Like something sharp blowed into me eye . . .

BENGRY *watches* JOHN *see to that. Then:*

BENGRY. What are you thinking, Samuel?

SAMUEL. The ocean, father. The many colours of it. And how it eats at the island all round; like a jigsaw-edge.

BENGRY. Why does that happen? Samuel?

SAMUEL. Some rock is softer, father: the sea more easy breaks it, to carry away. This could be not a island at all. But Sinbad's whale. A great eye open in the rock there. And all the island turn bottomside-up wi' us, and plunge to the bed of that deep.

BENGRY. What do you see, John?

JOHN. Father? I never saw stone so black as this. Gabbro . . . Dolerite . . . Belched burning from the belly of the world. Now this cold stone.

MICHAEL. There's volcanoes men only cod themselves is dead. That sudden wake.

JOHN. Ay. Earth's crust we stand on 's no thicker to her size than its peel to an apple. Beneath is magma and fire.

MICHAEL. If I lep, I might make a crack in the stone, an' fire flow out.

SAMUEL. When do we begin our tasks, Father? Our tasks ye promised us? The island our schuil, in it each of us his book? Mike the flowers, me the shore, John the rock?

MICHAEL. No time, the autumn, to go findin' flowers . . .

SAMUEL. Father? Father? Ye tremble.

BENGRY. Ay Samuel. Look at your sea now. And from the sky, look, all light going.

MICHAEL. Da? The quarry has stopped.

Silence indeed.

BENGRY. Cape Yell, look.

SAMUEL. I see no sea at all now.

MICHAEL. Sir Wendell's fortress, Da. Vanished. The soldiers. The Wall —

SAMUEL. Island gone, Father. Swallowed. This fog came sudden.

BENGRY (*quiet*). Yes.

Afar, long low swelling C of foghorn, darkly cloaked, falling at last to a dead all-but-pitchless A-stroke.

BENGRY. Let me button your jackets. Michael, Samuel. Up to your throats. All good boys must come to school.

MICHAEL. Lessons, Da? Now?

BENGRY. Your books.

SAMUEL. Now, Father?

BENGRY. Hurry.

MICHAEL. But —

BENGRY. Hurry!

SAMUEL. Father?

JOHN. Ye heard what he toul' ye! Down!

MICHAEL (*grumbling, clambering away*). How shall I find flowers in fog? In this thick fog, how shall I see anything?

SAMUEL (*likewise*). The shores is dangerous in fog.

BENGRY (*inly flailed*). John does not argue! (*Foghorn.*) Down after them, then, eh, John? Your jacket too. Careful.

JOHN *smiles back at him; gone.*

Our sons are never altogether ours. Angels only, loaned us a little while: for our mean fathering. Strangers: from some further shore . . .

Fog: through it, chapel bell here, school bell there, warning; their rhythms, pitch anomalous.

SISTER CROY. Una! — Davey! In, child, uir the Fog King'll get ye! — Una! (*Angst-ridden, haunted.*) Una! In! The Fog King'll get ye!

Foghorn muted afar.

Una!

Stoneyard: fog. YESCANAB *working with mallet and chisel,* CHILD MANATOND *pestering him with childish foghorn sounds. Chapel bell, school bell beyond.*

CHILD MANATOND. In, Stephen chil' . . . Uir tha FogKing get ye!

YESCANAB. Ay. (*Then.*) Heir's yuir father . . .

CHILD MANATOND (*desirous*). Daa . . . ? Daa . . . ?

MANATOND (*wheeling self*). Away outa the yard, you . . .

CHILD MANATOND (*loving*). Daa. Ma'n father's face is the sun in the sky . . .

MANATOND (*revolted*). Hands off of me!

CHILD MANATOND. Take me in yuir house, mine Da! (*Foghorn afar.*) FogKing walks, A'm afeared o' the King!

MANATOND. Their's no king . . . (*Struggling, thrusts* CHILD MANATOND *from him.*)

CHILD MANATOND. Daa . . . ! Daa . . . ! I love mine Daa . . .

MANATOND. In mine stoneyard indeed was this cross made. Outa this! Away. Till Sister Duinhead's house.

CHILD MANATOND *whimpering goes.*

Stephen.

YESCANAB. Sir?

MANATOND. Tools away for now, lad. An' away yuirself. Stephen. Home.

YESCANAB (*stowing implements away*). 'Home'. Wheir's that? Skew Yescanab has ways to go. Dance how his fiddle's tuned. This fog's mine element. (*Takes out from a hiding place a soldierpack.*) Across the island, ma cruiked road. Toward Sir Wendell's harbour. Ships lies there. Aboard. Below. Down among the cargo lie. Play stone, an part A've practised well enough. Away: across that water . . . Landfall, whatever Nineveh the Lord's marked out. Then: Christ mine Guard an' nethers ma guide . . . A'm shitin' Bibles at the thought. World Outside . . . Devil A don't know, better nor Devil A do.

Foghorn afar.

Trumpet o' Judgment? Well. Here comes I.

Act Two

Fog still; weedsuck, rockslap — a dark shore. CHILD MANATOND *muttering. Suddenly* SAMUEL, *high-satcheled, head weirdly seaweed-crowned.*

SAMUEL. Grrr! Grrr!

    CHILD MANATOND *grunts in dread, heaves, flailing.*

SAMUEL. Grr grr!

CHILD MANATOND (*becomes child, giggling in terror and delight*). Hee hee hee! Sahm! Sahmu Ell . . .

SAMUEL (*growling*). I'm the dragon. You're the princess. I rise from the vasty deep to swalley ye alive.

CHILD MANATOND (*laughs like a child*). Dee it again! 'Grr grr': make at me 'grr grr' again. Hee hee hee!

SAMUEL (*growls, devours, snaps*).

CHILD MANATOND (*titters, shrieks, mixed terror and delight: suddenly, mother-persona intervenes*): Sheela! Ahind ma this minute Sheela: down! (*Child:*) Maa . . . ? (*Mother, black:*) Si-lent. (*Pause. Nonself, stone, void:*) Shuidna be out, Child Samuel. Fog.

SAMUEL. Nor you shouldn't be out, if I shouldn't be out. Us both is out together.

    Foghorn, muffled afar.

CHILD MANATOND (*new persona: benevolent elder sister, gentle, pleading*). Help my sister. Help my little sister, please.

SAMUEL. Sister?

CHILD MANATOND. Help my sister. Sometimes she needs to go to the lava-tree. Must wet herself, is times. Cannae help it. Sahmuel. Speak till her nice.

SAMUEL. Sister? Yui? Yuir big sister says I'm to speak to ye nice.

CHILD MANATOND (*child*): Nice ta ma: mine big sister. She speiks ta ma nice. Married. Gone till Ireland . . . (*Lapses, almost autistic.*)

SAMUEL. Sister? Little Sister Manatond?

CHILD MANATOND *makes a childy wheedling snuggling sound.*

Look. Look at these. Seaweeds. Sugarwrack. Laminaria saccharina. That's a Latin name. . . . Tawse-weed. To mallavogue ye. (*Careful.*) Thrash thrash . . .

CHILD MANATOND: *child, comes giggling toward life.*

Eggweed. Look. Fat green eggs. Never burst: however much ye crush them. Try. (*Pause.*) Touch.

CHILD MANATOND (*hesitant sounds; then a flinching gasp, as from an electric shock; explodes into crazy tittering*). He he. Flower.

SAMUEL. Nor even wi' yuir teeth, can't burst them. Sister. Try. Tickle tickle. Tick tick tick . . .

CHILD MANATOND. Tickle. Tickle. T — . . . (*Sudden retching, spitting: mother again.*) Dark mahn, Sheela. Come out the deep to tempt ye. Filth-things in his hand.

SAMUEL. Seawrack only: that the tide brought in —

Sluggish wavebreaks encroach meanwhile.

CHILD MANATOND. Tide, ugh, ugh. Vomit, monthblood; foul; vile — (*Retching.*)

SAMUEL. That's no way to speak of the deep.

CHILD MANATOND. Duina lissen, Sheela! Lies. Lies. (*Child:*) A duina lissen. Lies! Lies!

SAMUEL. The deep is lovely. Splash splash. Oh Sister Manatond, repent an' be baptised! Splash splash — Just ye walk in the fetch of it a step or two, good sister. Take my hand . . .

CHILD MANATOND *is torn between attraction and dread.*

Why, what's to be afeared of? I have guid instinct —

CHILD MANATOND (*voices kaleidoscopically splinter, a babel of selves*). Ma! Ma! — Da! — Ma! — Sebastian! — Sheela-daughter! — Da! — Son! — Sheela-daughter, Sheela! (*Child, screaming, gone . . .*)

SAMUEL. Come back you! Foolish sister! (*Seafetch combing, dark.*) Sister . . . ? I didn't mean to afear ye. I'm sorry . . .

Foghorn afar, almost a ghost of itself, the fog so thick. A shape there, where CHILD MANATOND *went.*

SAMUEL (*approaching, hesitant*). Sister . . . ? Poor frightened
sister. Yui shuid not be afeared. Take you my hand —

*But what he brings down is not Child Manatond. A
pastor-figure, robes rent, face crazed through some terrible
experience; mouth mouthing, throat racked, gasping, dry.*

Who are you? Let go of me —

*The pastor-figure seems to be trying to tell him not to be
afraid.*

Pastor . . . ? Scarweth — ! Yuir tongue cut out — (*Suddenly he
is screaming, screaming, but his mouth is stopped by*
SCARWETH'S *clamping hand.*)

SCARWETH, *with his one hand, forces the stifled* SAMUEL
down: with his other, writes in the sand.

'Not drowned . . . The nineteen . . .'

But before he can ask anything SCARWETH *has him listen:
eldritch fragments of sound — someone somewhere quietly
tapping a tin or a jar with a stick or a pebble; someone else
there blowing a long high shrill obsessive note on a screamer
or pipe; muted dark deliberate rhythmic strokes on a flotsam
oildrum there . . . These fade and surface through the sea's
dark comb, suppressed and sinisterly luring: lost in foghorn,
eerie now, as* SCARWETH *bringing* SAMUEL *there . . .*

Fog still. MICHAEL, *high-satcheled, descending backwards on.*

MICHAEL. So much for the great Sir Wendell's mighty Wall.
(*Looks around him.*) The Master's Ground. . . Ahoy! A'hoy'i'
hoy'i'ho! Hi Bain. Is Bain at home?

*Cautious at first, then whistling, kicking, more noisily
explores. Foghorn, somewhat louder, clearer: nearer here.
Soon:*

Lord but look close. (*Eyes to ground; soon kneeling.*) Lichens.
Green beards, like of wee men frozen in the stones . . . The
brine sows these. The wind flails in the spores o' these across
the deep . . . And orange lichens; like blooms of rust . . . And
white . . . And grey . . . (*Starts to cut away at the stone with
a knife from his satchel.*) Our father's right: the more ye look,
the more its life appears . . .

He works away, whistling a hymntune, 'On Jordan's Bank' or

'Hail to the Lord's Anointed'. Thickening through the surrounding silence, a breathing rhythm, tidal, vast; an heartbeat, soft, colossal. Towering above him in the gloom, a titan form, in robe and crown of a king, its face a mask, with ravening mouth.

KING (*his voice given extra bass and resonance by personal microphone-devices about him, that amplify also his breathing, heartbeat, and every movement-sound he makes; his voice itself is soft, the island accent purified*). Child . . . ? Boy? Boy — ?

MICHAEL (*raising hands, helpless, petrified, as KING enshrouds him in his towering grasp*). King . . . ?

KING (*ghastly soft*). Ye trespass . . . Ye anger me. Ye find me at ma work . . . (*Voice caressing, needful, gentle.*) Come to my castle, little man. Pitta-patta, rabbit-heart . . . Soon be still . . .

MICHAEL. I dream this . . .

A THIRD FIGURE (*looms searching beyond*). Majesty . . . ? Majesty . . . ?

Foghorn; KING faltering as though at some response inbuilt in him to this. MICHAEL, clawing and stabbing at the royal face, finds it tearing away in his hands.

KING (*in mortal wound*). Ah . . .! Hands off of me! Our Royal Face . . .! (*Staggering, his huge hands clapped before his naked features, he pivots away.*) Holst . . . !

THIRD FIGURE (*seeing him, lovingly staying him; gentle, seductive, dangerously crazed*). Majesty . . . ? (*This HOLST an obscenely alarming figure: a pornographic 'black angel', ikon of bestial malehood, threatening sexual havoc to the world.*)

KING (*face smothered still*). Oh Holst . . . Holst . . . Our Royal Face . . .

HOLST sees the damage.

An child here . . . Manchild . . .

But MICHAEL, with the mask, is clambering away, up and along wall. HOLST must postpone all thought of that: the poor KING's wounded head, stripped of its royal self, the face, must be attended to.

HOLST (*caressingly*). Majesty . . . Come down into Your Kingdom Sir . . . (*Almost a whisper.*) Come down . . .

Foghorn: almost in response to which the KING must stand, royal as he can, one huge hand still covering his nakedness of royal self. HOLST brings him away.

Fog still. A new bellsound: fogbuoytoll, on restless sluggish water, irregular. YESCANAB creeping cautiously down in with soldierpack.

YESCANAB. Sir Wendell's harbour. Sleeps. Its thick grey shroud. Dead island's deader end. Well Yescanab. Join here the noble company of emigrants.

Slow flashing through gloom beyond: an orange foglamp. Soon another. TWO FIGURES there, guardlike, routinely quartering.

Soldiers? Here?

Guardfigures approach, turn, move away. Their uniforms are none that we recognise though each has the single chevron of Lance-Corporal. Something about the appearance of these also is sexually potent, though nothing so extravagantly as with HOLST.

Sort of soldiers? I been sleepin'. All this lively hope on ma own back duir . . .

Would be drawn aside cautiously after them but around him the scene is gradually peopling with a sense of activity. An expressionless murmuring, clarifies as a young woman's Cambridge voice reading down a consignment list; soon herself to appear, suited half-drab half-severe with a touch of scarf and one consistently straying lock of hair. With her a more elderly man, in black coat and black glasses, who onto documents of his own notes only the sparest occasional detail down.

WOMAN. . . . Avonmouth, England. Male, middle age. Category P, intake process normal, agent R-zero-three. Item, wallets, one; contents, driving licence, terminate; bank-card, terminate; photograph of presumed wife, reserve. Keys, small cash, cigarette-lighter, watch. No special characteristics. Two three one six nine nine zero three.

MAN (*makes a brief note. Then*): Yes?

WOMAN (*Next sheet*). Bridgnorth, Shropshire. Male, young, category Y, intake process complex, agents G-seven-two, R-five-nine. Item, penknife; wallet —

A sudden disturbance: whistle-blasts, a wild cry 'Man away!' A MAN; gagged, panting, hurtles on in desperate clumsy flight. He has been left with nothing but a loose pair of stained underpants. GUARDFIGURES swing round, pursue, brutally apprehend and fell him with almost pornographic gestures and postures: that sexual havoc here overtly threatened. Silence. Then GUARDS, with a third coming — some pornographic travesty of AN OFFICER, by uniform and accoutrement his male carnal havoc yet more threatening than theirs — dangerously encircle him. This officer we soon recognise as HOLST, in less ceremonial aspect here.

FIRST GUARD. Defector duly recovered, Sir.

A dark detonative stroke soon audible from now, at grim uninflecting 10.4 second interval, as from some distant subterranean depth. Fogbuoytoll, seasound intermittent, OFFICER kneels luxuriously astride defector; by a fine chain round his neck, on it a small metal disc, he is hauling up, up, the defector's head. The officer's own face seems somehow semi-idealised, personless, a masklike pornotopian smiling, the jaw's aggression emphasised.

OFFICER (*quiet, rural; reading the numbers imprinted on the disc*). Two-three-one-six-nine-nine-one-one? Didn't you like the look on us, then, two-three-one-six-nine-nine-one-one? (*He twists the defector's head round into wrenched unnatural postures to gasp up at each leering GUARD, their hands stroking hidden truncheons in their pockets there.*) What's your trip then, nine-one-one? What's your scenario? Defecting? Not to tremble, friend. It's glorious, our scenario for defectors. I'n't it?

FIRST GUARD. Yes Sir, glorious.

SECOND GUARD. Glorious, Sir.

Something about these figures is smouldering, a dangerous psychotic energy, any moment now to be tempestuously uncorked. They have soundlessly wrested the defector over onto his back, forcing his legs up, up, over his face, grouped tight around him. Grunts, gasps, as his spine is hooped and his legs yanked apart. Sudden disgust.

Ooh . . .

FIRST GUARD. Ooh . . .

SECOND GUARD. Look at this Sir.

OFFICER (*sees*). Oh . . . Abominable default in a man.

SECOND GUARD (*moronic snigger*). Defector defecator.

OFFICER. Loathsome.

*Black truncheon gripped strokingly in gloved fist now.
Suddenly, with easy movements and soft sounds, they are
bundling him away into the gloom to be about some obscure
business on him there.*

MAN. You are not mistaking this procedure?

WOMAN (*simple, factual, secure*). Doctor Nebewohl, one does not
come to the Skaranay station unqualified. This is presumably
already a controlled scenario. These 'guards' are Operatives:
the subject, without knowing it, has spontaneously selected a
function-role and activated the Programme on himself.

NEBEWOHL. Yes: in his case, a schema 'Deserter Pursued,
Recaptured, Purgatively Judged': over and over through this
schema experiencing his dysfunction: till what we strive for in
him. . . . Always am I wondering, should we not convey to the
subject somehow the ultimate — salvation for him to which
this apparent ordeal is the only path. . . No. In his terms, our
purpose would then seem to him the extinguishing of his
identity.

WOMAN. Identity?

NEBEWOHL. Miss Wenwood —

WOMAN. Wemwood, Doctor: w,e,*m*.

NEBEWOHL. The Identity might be a narcissist construct on no
existential base, we can agree that; but it is the quality of
hallucination to be experienced as real. Only through the
subject's delusion of an 'identity' can we function in him.
Hence, for instance, the pornographic mien of the Scenarios.
Either in Nature or the Laboratory, Evolution's no immaculate
conception.

WEMWOOD. I don't experience the issue in quite such

metaphysical terms, Doctor. The popular dogma of the Self, for all its mystique of Dignity, Liberty, is a romantic archaism that shackles Man in acquiescence in a slum and chaos of an earth. There will be *no* future, but for this minority of us with the courage to exercise a proper responsibility to the unborn. Item, wallets, one, contents, driving licence . . .

Moving away with NEBEWOHL.

The GUARDS *slowly ungroup, hauling the defector up onto his toes, to totter and hang there, eyes dazed in an incredulity that such an agony was possible as he has just endured.* OFFICER, *masklike jaw blankly smiling, wipes his truncheon on a handkerchief.*

FIRST GUARD (*gentle, nuzzling*). Down wi' us now? Nine-one-one? Mm?

SECOND GUARD (*likewise*). Down with us, friend? More below.

Like kindly nurses with a frightened patient they help him carefully away; OFFICER, *truncheon frogged, following, all officer again. Fogbuoytoll, restless seasound,* YESCANAB *surfacing; but that dark subterranean ictus audible still.*

YESCANAB. A thought I knew this place. 'Guid Sir Wendell': A begins ti wonder. Some pit the Master's House is builded on. Black crack in Skaranay's black underside . . . Back . . . ? Never. On . . . ? (*Pauses.*) Or be tempted aside a while . . . Down somehow . . . Follow ma nose . . .

Soothing wavebreak, backwash. Stillness, quiet; sunset light.

CHILD MANATOND. Mine heid is wide. Nine stone miles empty wide. Ma one heel on tha Sun, ma'n other awn tha Muin, A shite the earth. (*Obscene thrusts.*) Ugh. Ugh. (*Dangerously still, reduced.*) A ahm thon speckyspeck o' sahnd. Speck . . . Speckyspeck . . . Ff . . .

SAMUEL (*arriving, stunned, with satchel; self strangely weakened within*). Hi Mick.

MICHAEL (*likewise, opposite*). Hi Sam. Legion.

SAMUEL. Legion.

MICHAEL. How's all of you?

CHILD MANATOND (*mother, dark, defensive-aggressive*). This

child is closed. (*Child:*) I is not here. (JOHN *arriving.*) (*Mother:*) Ye's red about in this poor closed child's cracked crazy mind. (*Father:*) Son! Eft igh eft igh! (*Mother:*) This mi- Chi- Chai- Cloa- C- C- . . . (*Nonself:*) Yuis are stealin' mine voice!

MICHAEL. John?

SAMUEL. John?

JOHN. Mick. Sam. . . . Father?

MICHAEL. Da?

SAMUEL. Father?

BENGRY (*quietly arrived*). Well. John, Michael, Samuel. What did you learn today? John?

JOHN (*takes from the bag specimens of various rock as itemised*). The structure of this island, is an abomination of deformity. Two basic schools of rock make land. Volcanic: exploded burning from the earth; to cool and harden. Sedimentary: laid gradually down, wet dust of the sea bed; to harden. The various strata of each should lie, atop each other. But here. Here. Flagstone; lava; conglomerate. Millstone, andesite, jet, schist, ash: I find *beside* each other, dislocated, each appearing at the surface, side by side. Cause? The peculiar convulsion of this island's making. Deep inshock since.

BENGRY. Good. Samuel?

SAMUEL. Shells, Father. Seaweeds and shells.

BENGRY. Let's see the shells.

CHILD MANATOND (*beginnings of some crazy disturbance*). Ha ha ha.

SAMUEL. A razor shell. A necklace shell. Bugle shell.

MICHAEL. Ba pa paa! Ba pa paa!

CHILD MANATOND (*soldier-son persona*). Boo poo poo! Boo poo poo!

SAMUEL. Tower shell. Strange tower: corkscrew, pointed like a dart.

BENGRY. And this? Beautiful. Shaft, look, of ivory. Spiral. So delicate.

SAMUEL. Mm . . . (*Doesn't know.*)

BENGRY. Michael?

MICHAEL. Mm . . . (*Doesn't know.*)

JOHN. A —

BENGRY. Oh I know John knows. Mm? Wentletrap.

MICHAEL *snorts; whispers.* SAMUEL *giggles.*

All right, let's all share it.

MICHAEL. A Wendell-trap. To trap Sir Wendell Bain.

BENGRY (*waits for them to contain themselves. Then*). Here's a grim one.

SAMUEL. Urchinshell. The deep has eaten holes in it, Father. Let daylight in its empty skull.

CHILD MANATOND. Aa-a . . . Puir heid . . .

Seabreak a presence throughout . . .

BENGRY. Good finding, Samuel. Michael?

MICHAEL (*rooting in satchel*). Flowers, Da . . . Flowers. Ah . . . (*Brings out small specimens, squinnies at them.*) Eyesharp.

SAMUEL. Eye bright.

MICHAEL. Torment.

JOHN. Torment-ill.

BENGRY. This? (*A small yellow-spike.*)

MICHAEL. Aa . . .

BENGRY. This?

MICHAEL. Aa . . . Dark Doctor.

BENGRY (*amused*). Black Medick.

MICHAEL. Dark Doctor is a better name. Anyroad, it's yelley. (*He seems enfeebled.*)

BENGRY. This?

MICHAEL (*close, tired, unfocussed*). Jack-go-to-bed-at-twelve.

SAMUEL. At noon, you. Jack-go-to-bed-at-noon.

BENGRY. Something else you found, Michael?

MICHAEL. No, Father.

BENGRY. In your satchel something . . . ? (*Shakes it out; the king's mask.*) Forgotten this? . . . Mask . . . ?

CHILD MANATOND. Ha ha ha! An face wi'out an mahn!

BENGRY. Mask . . . ? Who here should need a mask, eh? Such a . . . mouth. . . . Where you find this, Michael? Michael.

MICHAEL. Me eyes is sore.

CHILD MANATOND (*childish*). I is an guid child. I hahs no name. Michael's an naughty girl: has an name, has an name!

SAMUEL. Poor mad sister.

CHILD MANATOND. Stone breist. Stone thigh. Stone head, stone heart. Stone eye. Ha ha ha, an mortal jigsaw! (*Tries clumsily assembling stones.*) Oh . . . wheir's fingers o' men, shall piece these out, to mek an picture of mine — self . . . ?

NEAND, SISTER DUINHEAD *are here, with an unhappy* MANATOND *wheeled by* YAGG; *and a vehement* SISTER CROY: *in delegation mood.*

NEAND. Pastor. The brotherhuid require ye, Pastor, to yoke these sons of yours within the discipline observed of all the rest.

YAGG. Let roam like savage beasts, wild-reared, wild-dressed: sews wildness in our children's heads. All children wuid be wild an' they were let be.

NEAND. Pastor they must come to school. Be dressed and disciplined like all the rest.

CHILD MANATOND. Ha ha. Mallavogue them. Thrash thrash. Thrash thrash. I'm a pig. Dangle all mine fifty elders out. Squeeze squeeze. Squeeze. Spit milk. Spit milk.

SISTER DUINHEAD. Sick damages yuir sons have done. She's ta ba left her lone: d'ya heir, d'ya heir?

CHILD MANATOND. D'ya heir, d'ya heir?

SISTER DUINHEAD. Striven sa hard have we, these years, ta tune some quiet in her mind. An' now it's all undone.

CHILD MANATOND. Ashoo ashoo, all fall down.

BENGRY. Is none to try, then, to make poor Legion whole?

SISTER DUINHEAD. Whole? Not all are called, Pastor, to be what ye term 'whole'. 'Whole', only theim as He Above will hahve be whole.

NEAND. Further. Pastor. The ceremony and our stewardship. Sir Wendell Bain requires — not requests: requires — that ye reinstate —

BENGRY. Sir Wendell Bain? Who has not condescended from his castle yet to darken my chapel door? Require? I reinstate nothing. I am your Pastor, not this Bain.

YAGG. Pastor. Yui forget. But for Sir Wendell Bain we'd none of us be here. We'd all abandoned our struggle long since, but for him.

ELDERS. Aymen, aymen.

YAGG. The squalor there was here, the barrenness, contagion; deaths of the newborn.

CHILD MANATOND. I died.

YAGG. The grave decision had been taken, Brothers, Sisters, quit or perish: leave this rock of our birth to wind and water and the birds. On that very eve of our migration, led by what pillar of fire we do not know, he came . . . And grafted us new holdfast here, never again to be bowed down nor driven off, but stand, work, proud against that element and that deep —

ELDERS ETC. Hallelujah!

BENGRY. He came to cut a quarry, Brother, not Tables of Stone.

YAGG. Yet also a Commandment, Pastor. Ay. In covenant to Him Above for our new life, to fashion of our dwellingplace a living mirror of His Purpose for mankind . . . Through Our Father's every chastisement of us, learn His Will: and carve from this mean rock a model of the Will on earth. In that inspiring, Sir Wendell Bain's authority lies: such words we never heard from Pastor.

BENGRY. No. Nor from me shall you not.

ELDER YESCANAB, *arrived meanwhile, leaden and burdened, bitterly takes his moment.*

ELDER YESCANAB. Well Pastor. Well. Yuir 'single stewardship' has proved too much for one.

BENGRY. Brother Yescanab?

ELDER YESCANAB. Yuir 'steward'. Mine son, sir. Stephen. He's nowhere to be found.

CHILD MANATOND. A've eaten him!

ELDER YESCANAB. His clothes are gone.

CHILD MANATOND. He's away in the heid!

BENGRY. Gone brother?

ELDER YESCANAB. What devil have ye called up in him?
'Pastor'? To have him turn his back on the rock of his birth?

BENGRY. His too, Brother, the grave decision, quit or die? Our
sons cannot be ours for ever. Our sons are gifts from God. Dark
though they burn, they come from Him and burn for Him
again. Our Lord Himself spoke of the sword He must bring
between father and son.

SISTER DUINHEAD. Blasphemer! Oh it is coming to pass, exactly
as guid Sir Wendell said. Our ordeals are His Trials of us. Look
and see! If we do not recognise. Shapes of our darkness: this
smiling Eli and his three black sons. Oh Wrath, sweet Wrath,
spin nearer, nearer, like an scorching sun: scorch, scourge an'
purify this festered place; burn this vile Satan out! Times, O
Lord, in fog and night, I, mine lone, closed in mine house by
my lit lamp, feel how I hear Your Tread tread toward mine
dwellingplace, Your Heartbeat beat, deep in the belly of the
rock, Your Breath breathe on mine bowed head. Oh sweet
dread King, be soon. Your Servants cry.

BENGRY. Put oil in your lamp then, sister, if you would be wise.
(*Only now does he unleash some elemental fury in him so far
pent.*) Elders? Deacons? Wicked husbandmen more like.
Gather about His Vine, to smite His Servants down! What God
is this you worship? One of love? No. All I hear is Wrath, Wrath.
Only His Chastisement can transfigure you? God? God? UnGod!
Covenant, 'model for His Will on earth' — each face like
stretched on the torturer's last? I come to tip this painted
tabernacle upside down!

ELDER YESCANAB (*quiet*). That ye'll never. Step out: who'll
bring this Satan bread to eat. Step out. Whui'll bring him meat
or bring him water. Step out. Whui'll take from his desecrating
hands the Bread and Blood. Step out! (*Silence.*) Chief Elder
Neand, our pastor again. We'll meet in secret houses. Let Satan
howl between his empty chapel walls.

Gathering around NEAND *they begin to move away into the
darkening twilight.*

SISTER DUINHEAD. Sister. In. Sister.

CHILD MANATOND. Sister me no sister.

SISTER DUINHEAD (*unbelieving, almost disvoiced*). What . . . ?

CHILD MANATOND. Duinhead. Dunghead.

SISTER DUINHEAD *speechless, unselfed.*

A spit ye out.

*Spits at her; soon is driving her away with stones. A pause.
Night is coming; the sea is heard. BENGRY and his sons stand
on alone.*

MICHAEL (*bleak*). Me eyes, Da.

BENGRY. Michael?

MICHAEL. Me eyes is sore. Like twin wee pins in the pupil of
each eye.

SAMUEL (*surprised*). Father I'm cold . . .

BENGRY. Samuel . . .?

SAMUEL (*shivering*). Father so cold.

CHILD MANATOND *is lurking on the fringe of them again.
BENGRY looks at his poor sons.*

BENGRY. John. In.

JOHN *like a mother brings MICHAEL and SAMUEL away.
CHILD MANATOND shyly follows them. BENGRY bleakly
watches. Alone, in darkness; quiet:*

Alleluia.

Part Two

The Pit

Act Three

Muffled afar below, that detonative ictus in the earth, its black stroke falling ever at that grimspaced uninflecting 10·4 second interval. But we are receiving its shock-vibrance now: subterranean darkness, NEBEWOHL *and* MISS WEMWOOD *arriving down onto a gallery above.*

NEBEWOHL. At this great depth in the earth we now arrive, it may seem paradoxical to say so but I am hoping that your head is good for the heights.

MISS WEMWOOD. My head is very steady, Doctor. It has needed to be. The landscapes have been quite vertiginous; in more senses than one.

NEBEWOHL. The landscapes from here on down are even more vertiginous.

MISS WEMWOOD. One had heard the model was functioning, but no conception how . . . totally . . .

NEBEWOHL. It is a prototype. But I am not without a certain . . . thaumaturgical pride in it . . . — Reveille. Look. Already the rock is coming alive.

He is hearing a sound that at first we do not: a high, delicate, probing whine stealing imperceptibly in upon the ear. This reaches a peak, then steeply decays. Repeat.

MISS WEMWOOD. At four in the afternoon, then, their day begins here?

NEBEWOHL. Also it is a shorter day for these: much shorter. Where no sunlight, where is time. These have forgotten the sun.

The rock is coming alive: feet first, iron and golden figures slowly thread themselves out; slowly, mechanically rise to stand clumsy, making vague atrophied gestures of self-cleaning.

MISS WEMWOOD. You've set them free from the circadian rhythm?

NEBEWOHL. But not altogether from the lunar: once each month still, in the waters of the tissues of these, the ghost of a lunar tide.

Eyes ever to the ground, arms slack, curved hands vacant, the

*iron figures slowly, almost blindly constellate themselves
around one golden one: from what in this gloom we can see of
their faces, all person gone. A new sound: lifelessly stimulative,
a dull scooping. Through the iron and gold figures begins to
run some gearing-up toward mechanical action. Treated
versions of* NEBEWOHL's *own pre-recorded voice erupt
refracted everywhere: 'Hurry! Hurry, my children! To your
workplace, hurry! You will lose your workplace, hurry!' The
figures raise blank heads: the sound of him transfigures them.
In a terrible joy they are hastening clumsily away.*

MISS WEMWOOD. It could not be defined as obedience, so much
. . . Nor even altogether as enslavement . . . The myth of you
as technologue of tyranny could at first seem vindicated: all
the appearances of a Platonic fascism are superficially
present . . . But for this joy. This transfiguration . . . Their
equivalents above in the streets show no such joy.

NEBEWOHL. In terms of Freudian technology it is an evident
equation. One is sublimating a Pleasure Principle altogether
into Reality Principle. Reality is what is. It is the only moral
political act: to fuse man into integration into this Reality,
and in experience of joy. Watch now the night shift putting
themselves to bed.

*Similar figures, dust-caked, slumped, come shuffling, drained
as by exhaustion of all will.*

The body-posture you might assume depressed from exhaustion,
is not so: but through withdrawal from their joy . . .

*Head first, face up, each iron figure is threading himself back-
wards into the rock, the golden figure with blank atrophied
parental gestures seeing them safe.* NEBEWOHL's *pre-recorded
voice now gently eases them: 'There, soldier: sleep. Sleep.
Quarry, sleep; quarry, sleep . . . Gentle, into your home in the
rock, just soldier-size. Sleep. I promise you: the voice of the
day shall come to you. You shall arise, to joy again.'*

MISS WEMWOOD. The trust of it . . . To lie there, threaded in to
that solid rock . . . All that weight of stone upon one's mouth
. . . I am chastened, Doctor. I fall far short of the equanimity
of that.

NEBEWOHL. These can experience no anxiety. Until the
Reveille sound, they feel in themselves no impulse to make

move of any kind. Also, this pulse in the earth, like a chthonic uterine heart, is soothing them.

All iron figures are vanished into the rock now; only the golden figure solitary remaining.

MISS WEMWOOD. What dreams do these have? This man for instance. Has he any memory of the scenario above? The schema, whatever his was, of delinquency and purgation through which he graduated here however long ago: does any trace persist of that? As the matrix of his dreams? But if that's so . . . I'm sorry, Doctor. I'm all questions. But you've broken through so many boundaries here, I'm in a behavioural territory quite without maps.

NEBEWOHL. Our monitoring reveals no trace of dream-activity. It would seem the old image-factory is quite empty: even of schema. Only one dream in them now: the one same dream between them all. One they carry, while they wake. (*Operates some intercom device, the golden figure responding to* NEBEWOHL's *now directionless voice as though to a voice heard transfiguringly in his head.*) Golden Soldier . . . Golden Corporal . . .

GOLDEN SOLDIER (*voice bleached, personless*). Father . . . ? Speaking to *me* . . . ?

NEBEWOHL. What is your name? Golden Corporal, tell Your Father your name.

GOLDEN SOLDIER. C- (*Blank, mind blank of all sense of it:*) C-orporal Gower. Father.

NEBEWOHL. Tell Your Father: what rank are you?

GOWER. Gold. Father.

NEBEWOHL. That is an high rank, Corporal Gower.

GOWER (*slightly triggered*). Gold does not speak to Iron except to say, Iron, do. Iron does not speak up to Gold, except to say Yes Gold, I Iron obey.

NEBEWOHL. Tell Your Father: why do these soldiers sleep?

GOWER. To give them strength for their tomorrow's joy.

NEBEWOHL. Describe this joy.

GOWER. All of us, numberless in this world: to hew this Palace of His Glorious Majesty from the rock: till it be finished and the King reward us. (*Catechistic but with bleak ravening passion.*) Life, life, our life our love: to carve and chisel, burnish, fashion, polish: His Dwelling Place: till it be finished and the King reward us.

NEBEWOHL. What do you expect, my son? What do you look to? when this King reward you?

GOWER. Why, Father, to be called above. Up: into . . . P-aradise . . . ! Each in his turn shall hear the Great King say *'This soldier's work is good, now call this soldier to Our Royal Side in Paradise for making into Light.'*

MISS WEMWOOD. This really stops me in my secular tracks: that you graft a *monarchy* into the model. One appreciates the elegance of the solution in a repressive context, for instance: the fount of honour in the inferno, as it were. But with a sublimation so self-ordaining and so pure as here, where is the functional need for such a myth?

NEBEWOHL. These eat still, these excrete still. They still have their anality to wrestle with. Now understand the logic of the process above: that inflammative assault on the dissonance the subject feels, between his narcissist 'self' and his lower function. He yearns for elevation upward, all of him. In the myth he is promised that: justification through work; to ultimate sublimation, through his King his Mediator into pure light. Even their recreation, games here, are all naive enactments of this alchemical scheme: *'I am King, this soldier's work is good . . .' 'No, I am King, this soldier's work is good, now call him . . .'* And always, for *'making into light'*. (*Through to* GOWER *again.*) Corporal Gower. Who is this King?

GOWER. He is the King of Love.

NEBEWOHL. You have seen Him?

GOWER. Father! Sometimes He comes down among us in this world. He walks in the world.

NEBEWOHL. Describe Him.

GOWER (*bleak*). How should a soldier look on Him? He is all Light. The sight of Him will blind a soldier. Until . . .

NEBEWOHL. Until?

GOWER. Until He call us into Paradise above, ourselves for
making into Light. At my last day, the King of Love shall look
upon the work of Gower and pronounce it good, and say 'This
soldier's work is good, I call it good, now bring him — '

NEBEWOHL *cuts him off, leaving* GOWER *mouthing
ecstatic and unheard.*

MISS WEMWOOD. The Myth walks? You've someone performing
this role? Physical, vulnerable: isn't there some incalculable
hazard for them here?

NEBEWOHL. The King is not like these. He is not a product of
their process. In fact he is an islander.

MISS WEMWOOD. From outside the system?

NEBEWOHL. An islander I find here, with a dysfunction that
qualifies him, perfect for the task. It was my solution, to
certain logistic difficulties I encountered. It operates
immaculately. Well. Kings come, kings go. It is only a robe
and a crown . . . (GOWER *stands waiting for His Father's voice
to come to him again.*) The King, besides, has also another
function. Remember the Operatives above, through whose
purgative labours there this Gower is here and in the joy he
is. Where all is bleached, the blackness must run somewhere.
Where is the Operatives' transcendence? From their deepening
burden from the duties they perform, to what expiation can
they look? If not from that same King of Love. Themselves
His Scapegoats: they soil their secular gloves, to keep His Royal
Gloves unsmirched. In the Royal Service has to be their perfect
freedom too.

MISS WEMWOOD. It is disturbing that one has not succeeded in
transcending *guilt.* You have constructed a system unprecedent-
edly pure; yet with both your bleached and your black, the
fulcrum of the structure seems still to be guilt.

NEBEWOHL. I can use only the architectonic principles the
world itself has furnished me. I could invent fantastic ones.
But it is in the world we live. From the world my data. Back
into the world my work is purposed. — Gower. Sleep now.
— Down.

NEBEWOHL, MISS WEMWOOD *are continuing down.*

MISS WEMWOOD. Still further?

NEBEWOHL. Yes, you must cross above the workface. The

Palace itself: which of course by definition can be never finished. Wear these now, we go down into the Chasm, and the sound is deafening.

MISS WEMWOOD. How far down in fact does Sir Wendell Bain's acquaintance with the project go?

NEBEWOHL. No deeper down than any man's. He makes the safe conventional assumption: Restricted Area, here must be clever whitecoats at their subterranean work, upon some new abomination to help Great Britain recover the tatters of her lost hegemony in the earth. He sleeps easy.

They are gone.

Massive ictus of the pit comes suddenly forward now. GOWER is not going to thread himself into the rock to sleep; he has some other, guilty, purpose. Alone now, he goes to where, here, there, two of the vanished iron soldiers sleep; gives each a surreptitious signal in the rock.

GOWER. Ironman Blackie . . . Ironman Chuck . . . Ironman Blackie . . . Ironman Chuck . . . (*These begin to thread themselves out.*) Time to P-lay now . . .

BLACKIE (*lowslung, dull*). Corporal Gower . . .

CHUCK (*hollowed, craven*). Corporal Gower . . . ?

GOWER. Secret p-lace we found when we b-roke that opening in the rock . . . Ironman Blackie, down . . .

BLACKIE. Corporal Gower is bad.

GOWER. Gower is Gold. Cannot be b-roken . . . Down: Iron.

BLACKIE. Yes Gold.

GOWER. Chuck, down.

CHUCK. I Iron obey.

They move away, in a new direction; soundless, cautious to be neither heard nor seen . . .

New acoustic: pit-stroke more dulled by intervening rock. Cold subterranean flowing water. YESCANAB creeping blindly down toward sound.

YESCANAB. Oh down deep deep A mustha come. Yescanab Jonah, belly o' the 'big fish'; three days an' nights . . . ?

Strange light yonder? Where light there should not be . . . ?

Gathering in their guilty secret 'garden' yonder, GOWER, CHUCK, BLACKIE *begin amorphously to play:*

BLACKIE. I am King!

CHUCK. No, I am King.

GOWER. Chuck, Blackie, you are neither of you King. Corporal Gower is King. I am King. Chuck, you are our Mother; Blackie is our Child.

Forlorn vague gestures of lost tenderness . . . Suddenly the tableau of them breaks:

BLACKIE. Now I am King!

CHUCK. No, I am King!

GOWER. Blackie is King now. I am our Mother. Chuck is Child.

They re-constellate so.

CHUCK. Corporal Gower, what is Mother?

GOWER (*Pause*). Mother is a . . . soldier, who is . . . I say, 'Chuck is my child . . . '

CHUCK. What is Child?

GOWER. A soldier who is . . . I put my hand on his head. I say 'You are my ch— . . . '

Silent. Hunter-keen has heard something! . . . CHUCK, BLACKIE look where he listens: the dark shape of YESCANAB there.

CHUCK. Over there, Corporal Gower.

BLACKIE. In the water . . . It stands from the *water* —

GOWER. Quiet.

Moves to see, CHUCK, BLACKIE *scuttling* —

Ironman Blackie, Ironman Chuck, do not leave me! I stand.

Nearer, nearer . . . Pauses . . . A sudden strange whimper, uncomprehending —

YESCANAB (*sotto*). Soldier . . . ? Some sort o' soldier; an' afeared? Of me?

BLACKIE (*toneless beyond*). Corporal Gower what is this thing?

GOWER. Quiet, Blackie! Ironman Chuck: still. This comes to us across this water . . . We soldiers burn in that. This rises from it. This must be a . . . 'angel' from the King.

YESCANAB. Angel? No, friend. A am an mahn —

GOWER. . . . M-an . . . ? M-an, what is that . . . ?

CHUCK. Careful. Ironman Blackie.

YESCANAB. An — a man from the island.

GOWER. I land?

YESCANAB. Above.

GOWER. Above?

YESCANAB. In the world. Corporal Gower. Above.

GOWER. Above? World? This is the world. Above is Paradise. Ah: Paradise above, you call the world, because it is your world. He is an Angel from the King.

They kneel for his annihilating stroke.

Angel. Sir. We found this place by — By our — clumsiness, Sir . . . B-roke the rock and f-ound this . . . We come here only sometimes. When we should be — sleeping.

BLACKIE. Why tell him? Nothing is hidden from the King. His Great Love watches over everything we do.

GOWER. *Because* he knows, we have to tell him.

BLACKIE. Now the King can never call us good. But we must work for ever and for ever.

YESCANAB. No . . .

GOWER. We have hurt the King's Love. I have led Chuck and Blackie from His Love. Bad soldier.

YESCANAB. Oh ma poor men, what has been done wi' ye? (*Reaches to* GOWER, *from whom a flinching hiss as burnt* —) It's only a hand. Gower. 'll not hurt ye. Gower . . .

Suddenly the lifeless stimulative sirensounds scoop up beyond. CHUCK, BLACKIE *stagger bewildered into their reflexes as before. But* GOWER *no; and without him they are directionless, lost.*

BLACKIE. Quickly. Quickly.

CHUCK. Quickly. Quickly. We shall lose our workplace. Quickly. Quickly.

Finding GOWER, *constellate around him unresponding there.*

Corporal Gower.

NEBEWOHL's *electronicised voice erupts, myriadly refracted, all but illegible beyond the rock:* 'Hurry. Hurry. To your workplace, hurry' *etc.* CHUCK, BLACKIE *claw blindly at* GOWER *to move.*

BLACKIE. Corporal Gower.

GOWER (*focussing slowly*). Fa-ther . . . ? (*Suddenly hearing. Reflex-driven, torn.*) An-gel . . . ?

Suddenly hurries with CHUCK *and* BLACKIE *away.*

YESCANAB. I imagine these. Oh down deep deep A've come indeed and A imagine these . . .

Follows where they have gone. For a brief moment a pandemonium of percussive bondage to the rock there, subterraneously echoing; the massive ictor of the pulse itself swung vastly forward, reverberant and cavernous. YESCANAB *retreats, astonished at what he sees.*

Chasm . . . ? Full with them . . . ? in toil and bondage to the rock itself? King . . . ? Love . . . ? Father . . . ? What Nineveh is this, city of what desolation I Yescanab uncover here: prisonerhuid live-buried in this world's cold crust? I am here . . . Yescanab, Stephen . . . Deep well indeed. Come here, how . . . ? But here I am . . . And this gold Gower . . . Poor shell . . . Oh Lazarus . . . (*Almost weeps. An intention dawns.*) 'Angel': of the 'King'? If thon's the only road ye'll understand me by, angel of this king I'll be. Up, to bring you: careful of you: to where yuir living shuid be done.

Far inrolling breaker, vast; annihilant crash of it. Its clattering backwash. MICHAEL, *blind now;* SAMUEL *bringing him.*

SAMUEL. This is the stormbeach. Michael. Sit you here. Listen thon deep. Boys but it's wild. Them seas off Antrim was powerful fierce, but none so troublesome nor cold as these. Man dear, the beauty of the earth, to have such shores. Oh lovely shores . . . And look at the sand itself. This grain. In this one grain, all colours: grey, fawn, blue, gold. Imagine: in this grain of sand, another universe, world, sapphire sky, grey Skaranay and shore . . . Or *this* all: grain, finger, Samuel, shore,

Skaranay, world, universe: within another, great, *great* grain of
sand upon the finger of some titan Samuel — Here's a mahn.
Michael. Black coat. Black bicycles on his face . . .

NEBEWOHL (*already darkly with them*). Is this the blindling? Do
not run away, I have not much time. I am Sir Vendell's doctor.
I know your brotherhood refuse the ministry of doctors, leave
everything for your Lord to cure. Therefore am I not known
of this side your wall. So let this be an earnest of mine deep
concern: how out from secrecy I reach mine hand, to see
what can be done about this child.

SAMUEL. Why've you black bicycles on your face?

NEBEWOHL. To be not recognised.

SAMUEL. Well we don't know ye, so take them off. One pair not
to be recognised: what for these other pair beneath?

NEBEWOHL. Against the light.

SAMUEL. Can you give Michael back his sight?

NEBEWOHL. I can end his blindness. Poor boy. Poor eyes. Has
he seen hallucinations then?

SAMUEL. He seen true things.

NEBEWOHL. Like?

SAMUEL (*bleak*). A King he seen. In robes and monstrous tall:
his mouth gaped open like the jaws of Hell. And at his side
another figure of a mahn. Black legionary . . . And *I* seen!
The nineteen drowned, not drowned at all: along Sir Wendell's
shore there, play, and cry, and laugh: demented and deformed!
Oh Sir —

NEBEWOHL. (*Studies him. Then turns to* MICHAEL *again*). Is
there pain?

SAMUEL. Of course there's on him pain. I knows. We're twins.
This pain he has, it's like a redhot coil o' wire, throb in the
ball of each eye — Look for yourself, sir, how his left has
swelled up on him the size of a egg. His eyes has lasted him
only his first few years, and all his days to come, burned holes
in his head. Poor Michael mahn, tap tap, white stick, pity the
puir dark fella.

MICHAEL. You say I have no eyes, sir. I have ten. (*His fingertips
exploring* NEBEWOHL's *face; from* NEBEWOHL *an almost*

inaudible bestial hiss . . .)

SAMUEL. Is you a doctor for the eyes? I read in a book, there can be special doctors for the eyes: is you such?

NEBEWOHL. Smear the eyeballs with this.

SAMUEL. What's thon? It's pricey, ointments.

NEBEWOHL. Yes. And this has — The formula, look.

SAMUEL. Ah jee, argentum, silver. Powerful pricey, then. We've no money.

NEBEWOHL. I am a doctor. I have sworn an oath. I give it you.

SAMUEL. Kind.

NEBEWOHL. Once each night. Before he sleep. I show you . . . (*Guides* SAMUEL *how:*) So. So . . . So. So . . . Not to rub. But to leave the ointment time to work behind the eyes.

Pause; then suddenly from SAMUEL *himself a high seared cry of pain. From* MICHAEL *nothing: but the pain is there.*

Healing: is pain. Think, Samuel. Silver is rare. Not to tell your father. He would be angry, because of his religion.

SAMUEL. Our father —

NEBEWOHL. Which of you can say he knows your father? When your mother was sick, might not a doctor have saved her? (*Lets this sink in.*) You must let your father think his prayers have done this. But you will be brave boys. You, shall have done this. (*Parentally enfolding them.*)

Darkness. Pit-stroke rock-muted near. GOWER's *cavern, cold flowing subterranean river.*

GOWER (*fragmentarily, intermittent, in his voice the merest hint of a South Walian tune returning.*) Angel . . . ? Angel . . . ? — He was never here. — He was here. Chuck and Blackie saw him too. He was here. — Angel . . . ?

Why is my head — heavy, that he is not here? What is this, when I only — think of him, turns me — heavy yet . . . filling me with this . . . (*Quarries the word.*) reaching . . . ? I have only to think of the angel, and there comes this reaching in me . . . Angel . . . ?

I lie in the rock. I sleep. The angel comes to me. I — reach to him: so — full for him — I wake: and he is gone. I cannot turn. I am in the rock. I have to lie there, in the rock: till the Voice of the Morning comes to set me — (*Pauses.*) Set me — (*Pauses. He has no word for it.*)

Angel. What have you done? Cruel angel, to a poor good soldier. Trouble is in Gower now. And you are gone . . . !

YESCANAB (*beyond*). Gower.

GOWER (*not seeing*). A-a? Angel . . . ?

YESCANAB (*nearer*). Gower! . . .

GOWER (*clumsy joy*). Angel! — Thought you had left me . . .

YESCANAB. No . . .

GOWER. Thought you had left me in the rock! You have. You stand across this river on the other side from me . . .

YESCANAB. Gower. (*Seems somewhat discrucifying accent for* GOWER's *understanding's sake.*) Two things ye can do. Stay thonder: fixed. Or cross this water, after me.

GOWER. No . . .

YESCANAB. Follow me. Up. Through this rock of the world, Gower. Come with me.

GOWER (*miserable dread*). How?

YESCANAB. What?

GOWER. Waters burns. They ring the world and will burn a soldier. Our Father has warned us —

YESCANAB. 'Father'? This 'Father' is telling you lies!

GOWER (*tabu-appalled*). No! No!

YESCANAB. I stand in this water: does it burn me?

GOWER. How can a angel burn?

YESCANAB. A leave ye, then.

GOWER. No! (*Pause. Wild:*) Angel! Help me! Do not blame me there is fear in me. Help me.

YESCANAB. Bow yuir head. With this water . . . I . . . touch yuir head . . . Now tell me does it burn.

GOWER. Cold . . . ! Cold . . . !

YESCANAB. Step down. Into the waters. Gower . . . Trust me
. . .

GOWER. Ohh . . . Burns me, burns me.

YESCANAB. The cold of it, Gower.

> GOWER *metallously staggering.*
>
> Take my hand, give me your hand — (*Joy.*) Good Gower!
>
> *A new sound: harsh, hysterical, sirens begin to scoop, muffled by rock beyond: escape-alarm —*
>
> GOWER: *a panicked reflex —*

YESCANAB. No, Gower, no! The Angel has yuir hand and will not let ye go.

> *Now the electronicised voice of* NEBEWOHL, *myriadly refracted through cavernous echoing beyond: 'Soldier astray. Soldier astray'.*

GOWER. My Father! My Father . . . !

YESCANAB. Gower!

> *Sounds cut, as though straying soldier expected immediately to rectify his course.*
>
> Your Father, or your angel.
>
> *Stillness.*

GOWER (*brute brain working it out*). You come to bring me to the King?

YESCANAB. Follow me.

> *Movement of them now.*
>
> Up Gower . . . A long climb. To the world. Above. (*Sotto*) And hope to Christ when at last we breist the brink of it it shall be night. Or fog . . . Whichever shallnae shock this Gower till his death when he sees.

Cold day. Chapel bell, a funeral toll, continuing.

SAMUEL (*bleak, uncomprehending*). His spine arched up from his bed like a hoop. His hands was like claws. He tried to tear his eyes out with his nails. His breathin' was like a whistle. He layed a long time so. After a while, he eased; then turned till his right side; curled his knees till his chin. His breath was very shally now. Faint. Then came a breath, was followed by no breath. And on the bed, was yellow flesh.

Toll has ceased: the funeral has come.

BENGRY (*quiet, so barely dare he speak*). Careful, John. How we lay the coffin down. Not to slip into the grave yourself. On wet grass, buryin', easy done.

CHILD MANATOND (*nonself, clumsy; at them*): A ringed the bell. (*Comes.*) A brought him flowers. Woundbright. Eyewort. Jack till his bed at noon of the day.

SAMUEL (*impatient of her*). Them's weeds, Child Manatond. Sticks an' thorns.

CHILD MANATOND. Brought him flowers. Rat tat. Rat tat. Anyone at home? Michael, it's your sister here.

BENGRY. Well Samuel. You know how it's done. SAMUEL *lowers one end of the coffin into the grave.*

CHILD MANATOND. Ha ha! Hi, Michael Bengryson, I see ye thrui yuir duir. The crow's home, the crow's home!

SAMUEL. Now his head.

BENGRY. Don't worry, Samuel: we steady him, he shall not fall.

CHILD MANATOND. Spake ta ma nice. Did Michael. Cam fram Ireland. Wee kind brother. Spake tae ma nice. (*Pauses, on brink of appalling laughter.*)

Suddenly BENGRY *begins to fill the grave.*

JOHN. No Committal, Father? For our brother that is gone?

BENGRY (*at last*). The Day Thou gavest, Lord, is ended.

JOHN (*pause*). Then give him your flowers now, Child Manatond. Before we cover him.

CHILD MANATOND. There. There. Black Medick. Tormentil. There. Hahahaha! The Pastor has his garden now!

BENGRY. That have I. (*And suddenly he is going.*)

SAMUEL. Father . . . ?

But JOHN *stays* SAMUEL *from staying him. Silence.*

JOHN. In the beginning . . . In the beginning . . . this earth was

fire. Wrenched from the Sun in His spin, to a tilted . . . whirling
. . . Slowly, from outmost innerwards, began to cool; give
vapours off, hissing, scalding, that cooled in turn, and as they
cooled condensed, to a cold, damp, dense shroud, so cold, so
damp, so dense, the light and warmth of the Sun were occluded
utterly from this. Darkness. In which darkness, this slower,
slower turning sphere began to abate its incandescence, liquefy,
congeal, wax solid; hard: around the retreating heart of fire
this was, a cold shell; colder. Equally the vapourshroud: damper,
denser; colder, colder, cold in step with cold, the shroud with
the shell. Until, at that moment of change where it must
happen, the shroud — precipitated; and began to pour dark,
cataclasmic waters down, to pound upon this scarred and riven
lightless carapace this was, gulf to the brim each hollow, crack,
fault, chasm they found — Thousands, thousands of thousands
of years those primal waters lashed the earth. They made these
seas.

Silence.

Then came a time, the vapour-shroud was spent. Feeble, it
rifted; tenuous, it drifted away. The light of that Sun . . .
strayed through: upon the earth: and there were days. The
earth was born anew, a creature under Heaven in itself. And
each day waxed in warmth. And one such day, in the stillness
of that deep, a stirring . . .

Stillness. Silence.

CHILD MANATOND. (*Is about to weep. Stonelike, unmoving
there, knelt; inly to crack. Sobs rip from her. Tears break, well,
smitten into life — a racking that she cannot staunch. Then
strangely she speaks of her own tears.*) It's rain . . . Rain . . .
Feel . . . Warm . . . Rain . . . I cuid be the rain . . . Oh terrible
thing: ta be the rain; fall for ever . . .

SAMUEL. Oh Sheila Manatond, ye quare an' water Michael's
grave.

CHILD MANATOND (*child suddenly, desperate in dread*). Mam'll
see, Mam'll see . . . She'll see I wet maself again . . . (*Stumbling
away.*) Wipe, wipe, wipe, wipe . . .

Silence; then brutally covering grave, JOHN *brings* SAMUEL
away.

Bright cold sunlight. Sea distant, long slow shallow combing almost inaudible. Turnstones' frail tremulous fluting delicate afar.

YESCANAB. Come out from the cave now. Gower. Into the sun.

> GOWER *emerges, a handkerchief for a blindfold shielding his eyes.*

> Over this last of the rocks; let me guide ye . . . Easy . . . Boot before boot across the sand . . .

GOWER. Sa-and . . . ?

YESCANAB. Feel.

GOWER. So empt-ee. No sounds . . . (*Suddenly afraid.*)

YESCANAB. No, listen.

> *Seasound.*

> GOWER: *a flinching cry —*

> The sea, Gower.

GOWER (*blank*). The see?

YESCANAB. Many waters —

> GOWER: *a flinching hiss, regressive —*

> — that do not burn. And listen.

> *Turnstones' delicate fluting flickering in and past, away.*

GOWER. Strange voices.

YESCANAB. Turnstones. Creatures of the waters. They feed among the wet sand . . . Listen. They move through the air . . .

GOWER. Oh let me see.

YESCANAB. No Gower! Not yet awhile. Ye must keep this over yuir eyes — Against this light. Awhile only, Gower, A promise ye —

GOWER. Angel. I want to see —

YESCANAB. No Gower, not so soon. The sight of this Heaven shall be lovely, but not too soon or it shall burn ye. Gower. That have walked in darkness so long. Come Gower: we've a ways to go —

GOWER. Let me see! Let me see these things of Heaven — (*Clawing at the bandage.*)

YESCANAB. Gower — !

But already the bandage is torn away: from GOWER *a gasp of lightshock.*

From the Sun, Gower: turn your head! Face down — ! Not yet awhile . . .

GOWER. You stand so dark to me, against this — light . . . Black shape . . . (*The light sears him* —)

YESCANAB. Eyes not to raise yet, Gower, but around ye. To right or left of me, Gower. Sand, sea; world . . .

GOWER. (*Does so.*) Take me away!

YESCANAB. Stand.

GOWER. Back down into the world!

YESCANAB. This is the world.

GOWER. No —

YESCANAB. Stand. One step before the other. Walk.

GOWER. I shall fall.

YESCANAB. How 'fall'?

GOWER. All that is Heaven, I shall fall down through it for ever!

YESCANAB. Do I fall?

GOWER. Here is your home Sir. You are made for Heaven. You may walk across this Heaven and not fall. A soldier is — heavy . . .

YESCANAB. Look behind. So far ye have come, and not fallen. Only ye could not see: to be afeared.

GOWER *looks.*

Walk, Gower. Up on this track now. Quickly —

GOWER. You move so easy. Gower is so — c-lumsy . . . (*Stumbling after.*) Gower's gold was a — g-lory in the world . . . But in this Heaven. Beside — you —

And now YESCANAB — *and we — see the ugly personlessness the long years in the pit have done* GOWER's *face.*

YESCANAB (*revolted*). Oh Gower . . .

GOWER (*not understanding*). Angel . . . ? I am not the soldier angel came for? This soldier I am is — loathsome to him?

YESCANAB. No Gower . . .

GOWER. Gower is loathsome to the angel?

YESCANAB. No, Gower, I look at ye now —

GOWER. Corporal when you speak to me! — Someone else you came for. Someone not loathsome. Someone — worthy to stand in this lovely Heaven . . . ? Not this loathsome —

YESCANAB. No Gower. Not you: but what's been done to ye, is loathsome. Try to remember. How ye came here, Gower. Across that water ye came here: try to remember!

GOWER (*bitter refusing*). Remember, what is that?

YESCANAB. In your head, Gower: some picture you carry —

GOWER. Loathing in your angel's eyes: that I carry. Angel's loathing when he sees Gower loathsome in the light of Paradise.

The sharpness of the light is going.

Cruel angel, trick Gower up to show me all is lovely in this lovely world, but Gower loathsome . . .

YESCANAB. No — !

GOWER (*wild*). Hands off of me! Cruel angel, mock me; false!

Light thickening to fog.

But not the King: shall not be false . . .

YESCANAB. Oh Gower, no . . .

GOWER. Not my King shall not be cruel . . . Majesty?

YESCANAB. Gower, no — !

GOWER. Not my King, does not find his soldier loathsome. The King is glad in me. Majesty? Ha ha! False angel's empty Heaven's disappearing now!

Stumbling further from YESCANAB *in thickening gloom.*

Majesty . . . !

YESCANAB. Gower . . . ! Gower — !

Foghorn malevolent above.

GOWER. A! The King has hears! He answers me! Majesty? King of

Love? I hear you . . . ! You are very near . . .

Thickening now, the tidal breathing and the heartbeat of the
KING: *the looming, titan shape of him, cautious, apprehensive*
in his mended mask. Opposite, that other monstrous form:

HOLST. Majesty . . . ?

GOWER (*sees*). Oh. Majesty! My King! (*Hurls himself at* KING's
feet in joy.)

KING. (*Staggering back, hands protecting royal face — but some-*
thing loving-sonly in this figure's posture gives him pause —
and wondering . . .)

Holst . . . ?

HOLST. Sir?

GOWER. Oh how I love you!

KING. Holst . . . ?

HOLST. Majesty. Be still, Sir. (*Turns to a sick suppressed*
impotent contemplation of this golden figure; like a devil with
a pure soul falling from paradise, ravening to ravage him.)
Gold is a pure rank. How is this here?

GOWER. False angel came, Sir. Led Gower astray from the King's
good Love. Bad soldier.

KING. One of the bowing thousands? Stray? How? Yet stray, and
still come back to me? In his own love? Oh Holst. Oh soldier.
What is your name?

GOWER. Gower Sir.

KING. Oh Gower. Lost child, found again.

GOWER (*melting in ecstasy beneath the* KING's *loving hand*). Oh
my King. Oh my love my love my King.

HOLST. Hand off this, Sir. There is some blemish in this.

KING. Ay. That part in him that caused him stray. Oh soldier,
where's the pain? Here? Here?

GOWER. Oh . . .

HOLST. Majesty. Holst's task, this.

KING. Ay.

HOLST. Body of golden. Shoulder of golden. Golden soldierspine.

Hip of golden; belly; thigh . . . Somewhere in the kingdom of the gold some little crack, let this flawed matter out and lets Holst in . . . ?

KING. Ay Holst, the blemish must be found.

HOLST (*clamping himself to* GOWER *like some black bat*). Off with this fool's-gold. Unshell him. Peel him! (*Rending gold tawdry away.*)

GOWER. Yes! Yes!

KING. Ay Holst, we must set free his love.

HOLST. Oh some long time with us must this have been. Gravewhite, coffinflesh. So long, your chain quite grown into your neck, Gower — Up by it, up by it, up, up —

GOWER (*ecstasy*). Oh Majesty!

KING. Courage, Holst.

HOLST. Old number indeed. After such long purity to stray. Abominable default. (*Sotto*) Oh I would make such song in this.

GOWER (*seizing* HOLST's *hand*). Oh angel, heal me. Quickly. Oh my loved King —

HOLST (*separating* KING *from* GOWER). Majesty. Soldierbusiness.

KING. Kingbusiness too.

HOLST. Sir?

KING. We love this soldier. We'll not let him from our sight, till the pain in him is found and he is free.

HOLST. Oh Majesty . . .

KING. The King will share his soldier's journey into joy.

HOLST. Majesty, the song of a soldier on this journey's not — fit for royal hearing Sir.

KING. Royal? Royal? Oh Holst, ye'll royal me enough, but when did ye ever king us, ha? King me true: as Gower has? I was only a robe and a crown till now. (*Swaying somewhat. Foghorn.*) I will be true King in my Kingdom. Taste of it. True.

HOLST. Would you, Sir? Down among the soldierbusiness?

KING. Ay Holst. Gower, ye make a marriage of me with my Kingdom. This soldier's work is good!

HOLST. If that is your will, Sir.

KING. It is my deep will.

HOLST. Step down with us into your kingdom what it is, then.
    Majesty. (*Taking* KING's *hand also.*) Drink of it.

KING (*childish proud*). Ha: a moment of change, Holst. No?

GOWER. True healing angel! (HOLST *brings them away . . .*)

*Fog still, with sunsetlight. Foghorn farther off. Seasound, a
broken shore.* SISTER DUINHEAD *comes dragging* SAMUEL.

SISTER DUINHEAD. 'King'?! 'Black legionary'?! The nineteen
    Sabbath-sinly drowned not drowned at all, but lep an' scream
    on guid Sir Wendell's shore! Show them me. Child Sahmuel.
    Where are they, show me them!

SAMUEL. A King we seen. Them nineteen dance, I seen. Seen!
    Childer that's growed old yet's childer still, lep an' cry on this
    shore, demented and deformed. And a mahn. Black coat, black —

SISTER DUINHEAD. Ay. Ye hahve me almost afeared mineself,
    to lift mine eyes, wi'out A might dread to see this 'King' mine
    self! Afeared to use mine ears, for fear I might not hear yuir
    'twisted childer's' cries! Sick dreimin', of an sick sick child!

SAMUEL. I seen these, Duinhead.

SISTER DUINHEAD. Sister, to you.

SAMUEL. No sister to me, black abbess. Abscess! Haha, did no
    one lance ye yet an' all yuir pus-y bow'ls guish out? Judas-sister
    — ?

SISTER DUINHEAD *strikes his face.*

Slap me. I'm an Christian chil'. I turn me other cheek. Slapslap.
    Slapslap.

SISTER DUINHEAD. If it's like the cheek ye's have offered us
    so far, ye can keep it. Wha's thon yui're findin'? Give me,
    give me.

SAMUEL. Tha *were* heir . . .

SISTER DUINHEAD (*contempt, disgust*). An rooj-stick?

SAMUEL. Lipstick to you. From their blaspheemous games, one
    o' the demented an' deformed let fall.

SISTER DUINHEAD. Ye brocht it yuirself. Deceitful child. Sick child. Jezebel. Daub yuir boyface like an lass.

SAMUEL. Give me the lipstick, ye oul' black crow, it's avidence!

SISTER DUINHEAD. I'll give it ye. Samuel Bengry Pastorson. Wrong child . . .

SAMUEL. It's yui is wrong —

SISTER DUINHEAD. Wrong child, wrong child. (*Is scoring an obliterating cross across his face.*) Out. Out . . . (*Relaxes from him, spent.*) Carry that cross.

SAMUEL (*injured, weakened*). Cruel sister. Cruel till my brothers an' to me . . . These things is here! Ahn' yuis shuid want to know of them! For yuir own selves' sake!

SISTER DUINHEAD (*still*). Our 'selves': are in Our Father's hands.

She goes. SAMUEL alone, amid seasound a threatening presence now. Through half-gloom opposite two figures emerge. A BOY grown into something like a woman, face Babylonishly daubed. A GIRL made man, beating a tin with a stick — a sound we have heard before; her head by some embolic injection rendered colossal, lolling.

SAMUEL. Oh. Oh, brother, sister . . . Hi Duinhead! They are here! Come back yui! See! — Oh poor demented an' deformed. This time don't run away. I am only the pastor's son. I've telled me father yuis are here. Poor childer of Nineveh, in bondage and in grevious torment! But the prophet saith: 'Woe to the bloody city! Forty days, forty days an' Nineveh shall be overthrow — '

Foghorn, fog thickening again: seasound an inclawing annihilating force. SAMUEL sees the intention of these two upon him is terrible. And all flight barred. With NEBEWOHL have they come. He toys with his finger the rim of a glass: from this, a strange high intermittent note.

Hi. Yui. Lord of Night. I see ye who ye are! (*A wave crashes.*) No! No! Oh Children of Nineveh, help Samuel . . .

BOY-WOMAN. Sam, Sam, the pastor's son, gaes down till tha sea . . .

GIRL-MAN. Tap tap. Tap tap. Ta do his busyness in mighty waters.

SAMUEL opens his mouth. His cry is unheard. Sea-crash

engulfing him, black NEBEWOHL *obliterating him. Foghorn.*

Tap tap. Tap tap.

NEBEWOHL (*watching, farther and farther out*). Now once more
down: for only once more up again. This is your Samuel-Bengry-
death. Now down again: and never no more up again. They say
we bite our tongues off when we drown.

*Darkness. Pit-stroke a ghastly ghost afar. Dying flamelight. An
illegible human charnel, smoking still.* KING *inly undone; black
gleaming* HOLST — *his accoutrements bloodied and slimed — the
monarch now.*

KING. We have loved him out. Our golden Gower. He sings to us
no more. Oh Holst: ye reek of blood and of organs. This terrible
necessity, A never guessed. He should have loved his King:
better.

HOLST (*gently withdrawing it from the charnel*). Majesty. Your
hand. Sir.

KING. Ay. Wipe. Wipe. He hangs here, like the torn flames of a
Sun. The image of it, burned for ever on my mind. Holst, Holst,
after what A've seen ye have to do this night, A can never be
again the self A was . . .

HOLST. Oh Majesty, what self was that?

KING. Ha?

HOLST. All soldiers' deaths are owed to you.

KING. Take me away. Help me. Ma leigs. A canna raise maself . . .
Holst, help me to ma bed. A am sick with death . . .

HOLST. If you are sick of death Sir, you are sick of your Kingdom.

KING. Carry me.

HOLST. Ay.

KING (*cannot grip him*). Mine fingers . . . slide . . .

HOLST. I squat Sir. When I shit, I bury nations. Up!

KING. Oh Holst. Night stallion.

HOLST. Hold to your crown.

*Bears him away. In terrible silence, amid the charnel ruiny:
white, goldenheaded, pure, the primal essence,* GOWER
himself.

GOWER (*songless, stunned*). They have divided me. They clamped
me to a wheel, my face to Heaven, arms out, legs wide. Brought
whitehot blades: to ease between my hides: along my arms,
calves, sides, to slit me, long and parallel and deep. Here, here,
here; here, here; here, here, here . . . 'Search more', Holst said.
With the redhot piercing tips of hooks, the wall of my belly,
the flesh of my breast: deeper; deeper . . . the flesh ripped out
of me. 'Look!' they said, 'we can see his beating heart!' And
the King said: 'That? An heart? Is that what breaks in a man?'
'Caress him more,' Holst said; 'search more.' Everywhere that
I was rent and gouged, with seething oil and spitting pitch and
wax they larded me. So . . . So . . . So . . . My legs raised up
before me, up, over my face, to bend me like a hoop: there
into me . . . with a searing implement, opening me and pumping
into me such scalding shocks — How could I endure this? I
was fixed . . . Why am I in so many pieces? To each of them
that worked upon me, each an arm or leg of me: to jerk,
wrench, strain, each toward his own crossquarter with each
his part of me. But I would not undo, they could not even
split my fork. At last Holst said, 'we must ease him with saws.'
Holst hagged me, most careful; and while he sawed me through
my armpits and my groin, I uttered not one cry. Why was that?
I came apart quite easy then. (*Pause*.)

Poor King of Love. To find a soldier blemished. And have to
toil so hard and long unstitching me. That I should make him
weep, over whatever blemish Gower's was, in a beloved soldier.
Poor King . . . To make Him grieve . . . Poor King of Love . . .

Slow to darkness.

JOHN. Here's another, face on him long as a Lurgan spade. Hi Stephen. Did ye loss a gold pound an' found a penny?

YESCANAB (*beyond; a new private grimness in him*). Ay. Bad steward that A ahm.

CHILD MANATOND. Thought we'd lost ye.

YESCANAB *would say they have: but says nothing.*

Turned up again.

YESCANAB *says nothing.*

Poke. Poke.

YESCANAB. Oh Gower . . . Gower . . . What have I done . . . ? Mine ye were . . . Real ye were . . . Needing me . . . Not in some dream o' the night but out, real, other: self yuirself: reachin' out toward me from real darkness to be given life . . . Mahn, real, self, other, real: other, I was not equal to, but lost ye — Worse — Let fall down intill that pit again . . .

CHILD MANATOND (*weird clumsy impulse*). Here is an cloth ta wipe yuir eyes, mahn.

YESCANAB. Oh. Sheila. Mahn . . . Ay. Mahn I am. It's man I am, burns: to take man or be tuik by him: as man, to give man man . . . Give. There's a conundrum. To take must be to give. And to be taken, that must be to give. Equal. Oh Stephen from now, act right in the head.

CHILD MANATOND. I's a heid! We've heids all three. Here. Have one o' these.

YESCANAB. What's these Sheila? sweets?

CHILD MANATOND. Nothin's.

YESCANAB. It's a while since A clashed ma teeth in one o' these. (*Thoughtful mock-munching.*) Foolish Stephen indeed. Who ever till now thought his hunger could be fed on empty — figures o' the air. So how else then, than mine — my hunger as misshapen me . . . ? Go where I am. Seek where my bread or true life's to be found. Clever sister.

CHILD MANATOND (*conspiratorial*). My father's nowt but a hole and an heid.

YESCANAB. Off wi' his heid then, ha? — There's another, is real. Eh? Flesh, bone: man. Self: if self we can call it. John. 'In,

Part Three

Surrection

Act Four

Cold bright day. Stormbeach: tide-birds raucous, disturbed
beyond. Breakers, moderate; backwash pebble-combed. CHIL
MANATOND. JOHN, *apart, gathering driftwood into a barro*

JOHN. Cheer up, Child Manatond. (*No response.*) I'll tell ye
joke. (*Thick Ulster:*) I'll ask ye a condundhrum. (*Ordina*
voice:) Where in the Scriptures is the game of cricket pl
(*No answer.*) Acts two fourteen: when Peter stuid up w
eleven and was bold. (*No response.*) Who was the small
in the Bible? (*No answer.*) Bildad the Shuhite. (*No res*
The Shoe-Height. Build-Dad the — (*Gives up.*) I'll tell
amiss wi' you. You've no humour. How's this, then?
brother Michael's dayud. Och away, what did the pu
of? He died of a Friday. (*Silence. No joke:*) My bro
Sammy's drowned. He drowned of a Wednesday.

CHILD MANATOND. He cuidny float. He cuidny ri
One step up and two step down, and down he'll g
bottom of the drown. What an age in an child, to

JOHN. Ay Sister. Below Sam's gone. Down, down
reach of any light.

CHILD MANATOND. Wee kind Sahm, Lord shall
intil darkness.

JOHN. No Sister. What I mean . . . Look at the
of day cannot pass down through all the kin
deep. Two hundred fathoms down, the red
light goes out: deeper than that, only the y
green of it can go. Two hundred further fat
yellow goes out. Last, at seven hundred fa
green, that is all is left of the light, goes o
no light at all can pass. And there; deep;
deep's deep deepest deepest deepmost d
and endless night, the things that dwell,
light, are born without eyes.

Well. It was always the sea for Samuel.
must live.

CHILD MANATOND (*shaken*). Cold m

JOHN (*a terrible nigh-inaudibility, fire*

CHILD MANATOND. Mike, Sahm an
young.

child, uir the FogKing get ye': did ever ye hear that? (*Now it is* JOHN's *turn to say nothing.*) A King does walk. I have seen him. Monstrous. Thonder that wall, in fog: go down, into his — kingdom. And his kingdom nor he is nothing lovely. I have seen. How should you understand? A Pastor's son. While all yuir eyes is up to Heaven here, what filth's below. It's murky Stephen had the nose for that. The King went down. A waited. Soon or late I knew he must come up again. I waited. He loomed in the night. Like a drunken man. Mutterin'. I followed him. His dark road home: this way. By a old sheep pen he stopped. He stooped. Tuik off him. Robe; crown . . .

Of all men: to be him.

JOHN *says nothing.*

Of all men John: him: was so kind.

JOHN. Why me tell? Me, this? Tell my father.

YESCANAB. Yui — Yui're of an age wi' me.

JOHN. Oh. Age.

YESCANAB. Who else is safe for me to tell?

JOHN (*riven*). Oh John is safe. What Stephen knows is safe with John. John's no part of the corrupted world. Suppose — No. No, Stephen, imagine. An angel: sent down into this world: flame, to walk among mankind, in shape of man himself: deluded that he is a man himself. Poor angel: when deep in him the knowledge now begins to rise: he is not man like these; he is here but, only to burn. To touch this world of stone to life by virtue of the fire he is; never for him any partaking in the life he gives. His task, to burn beneath the sky alone: for others' — wakening. Think Stephen. That angel might walk this very shore. And if he met with a Stephen on this ocean's edge, Stephen a man, a Stephen blood water milk and clay: might not that angel yearn to give nine-hundred-and-ninety-nine thousandths of that infinity he is, for one day only of being Stephen's clay? That angel might gladly cry 'I give it all', for one short mortal sunrise-to-sunset day of being — Of being.

YESCANAB. There's nothing a Stephen could do. Stephen must go his way.

JOHN. And that's the angel's only joy: that those he touch to life, go from him, free. (*Resumes gathering.*)

YESCANAB. A spadeful or two o' seathrift 'll keep yuir fire in. Ye use it like turf.

JOHN works on. Still YESCANAB *does not go.*

I can tell you where's need of a sermon. John. And to a captive congregation. Need of an angel go down into a world of stone, touch it to life.

JOHN. Yes. Stephen. I know. A sermon I dread to give.

YESCANAB. You? Know? (*Suddenly so much he would ask: but in an instant this* JOHN *has magnified before him so, and his questions are all stilled.*)

JOHN. With your help, Stephen.

YESCANAB (*terror*). Us?

JOHN is suddenly bringing the barrow away: past CHILD MANATOND, *who has been daubing her face with a lipstick she has found, and is guirning at her reflection in a pool.*

JOHN. Ha. Look at this one. Afflictin' her countenance wi' rooj.

CHILD MANATOND. It is a lipp stick. Oh, I is beautiful! Diana o' the Ephesians, queen of breasts!

JOHN. Ye'd fifty breasts before, it's down to seven now, ye'll make a woman yet.

Moving away, YESCANAB *bewildered following.*

CHILD MANATOND. Oh . . . Little Sister Manatond, her lone on the shore. Sahd . . . (*Imitates tidebird-cries, delicate:*) Ssss . . . Ssss . . . Oh . . . Michael and Samuel, gone . . . No more play wi' me . . . Twin little monkeys o' the Lord . . . (*Strange keening:*) Micha El . . . Sahmu El . . . (*Suddenly, new voices in her:*) 'Mike . . . ! Mikel . . . ! Mikel, it's Sahm. It's Sahm, Mikel . . . ' 'Sahm . . . ?' 'Mikel. Who is here?' 'Why, her.' 'Who's her?' 'This lady on the earth.'

Night. SISTER DUINHEAD *comes, dressed in coarse nightshift.*

SISTER DUINHEAD. Mine lamp is in mine window. In this dark night the Lord shall not be lost. Mine lamp is here to guide Him if He come. Sister Duinhead's duir's not locked. Sister Duinhead's house is His. (*Kneels, sings in simple prayer:*)

Come, O thou Traveller unknown,
Whom still I hold, but cannot see:

My company before is gone,
And I am left alone with thee;
With thee all night I mean to stay,
And wrestle till the break of day.

I need not tell thee who I am,
My misery or sin declare;
Thouself hast called me by my name;
Look on thy hands, and read it there!
But who, I ask thee, who art thou?
Tell me thy name, and tell me now.

Silence. Darkness.

Pit-stroke vibrance muffled by rock beyond; cold flowing subterranean river. GOWER's *cavern.* JOHN, *robed as king:* YESCANAB *handing him the crown.*

YESCANAB. Well. John. Afeared?

JOHN. It rests with me now.

YESCANAB (*gives him the mask*). Away on in, then. 'Majesty'.

Shows him the way that Gower, Chuck and Blackie had once gone. JOHN *crosses down into the pit as king.*

The way to the tomb, I can help ye find. But down in to these heads, what road? (*He stands waiting, listening.*)

Chasm-stroke at full pitch, present. SOLDIER-FORMS *of all ranks slaving at the rock; somewhere the black* HOLST *eyeing them. The* 'KING' *coming among them, feeling his way.*

SOLDIERS. The King . . . The King . . . Soldiers: the King . . . The King . . . The King . . . (*Confused, falling in awe, heads bowed.*)

HOLST. Majesty? Majesty? Majesty, not this way Sir.

JOHN. Which way then?

HOLST. Why Sir, into your — This is not my King — (*Lunging at him with a bestial roar.*)

SOLDIERS (*triggered*). Holst reaches his hand against our King — (*They leap like automata to haul* HOLST *away.*) The King! The King! Protect the King!

HOLST *howls for wherever his true king might be, to hear.*

SOLDIERS *with mechanical unceasing press staunch smother him.*

Majesty . . . ! Help Holst! Majesty, help me — !

Only when he resists no more can they ease from him, a meaningless black shape.

JOHN. Oh soldiers. What was this?

SOLDIERS. — Him you most cherish Sir . . . — H-olst . . . Sir. (*The first of these seems* BLACKIE; *this second,* CHUCK.) B-ut . . .

JOHN. But?

The SOLDIERS *cannot understand why* HOLST *does not move . . .*

He is dead.

SOLDIERS. D-ead . . . ?

CHUCK (*blank*). Dead . . . ?

JOHN. Turned to stone.

With their 'King' they explore HOLST's *deadness, all —* JOHN *too in his own way — digesting the moral burden of it.*

BLACKIE. He whom the King most cherishes, we have turned to stone?

CHUCK. But . . .

BLACKIE. Now He shall never call us to His Royal Side.

CHUCK. Bad soldiers. But (*split, powerless, that a right action has proved also a bad one*) — But . . .

JOHN. Good soldiers. I did not cherish this.

CHUCK. Good . . . ?

JOHN. This was not my servant. This was the servant of another King.

SOLDIERS. Another King . . . ?

JOHN. The King of Death.

CHUCK. D-eath . . . ? King of D-eath . . . ?

BLACKIE. Another King . . . ?

JOHN. Two Kings. The King of Love . . .

SOLDIERS (*fervent*). Yes, yes . . .

JOHN. . . . The King of Death. It was the King of Death, cherished this. Good soldiers! Good!

BLACKIE. Another King . . . ?

JOHN. The King of Death: comes down into the world: to turn all men to stone.

SOLDIERS. No . . . No . . .

JOHN. To turn yous all to stone.

CHUCK. How Sir? Like we have done? To this?

JOHN. Slow. Slow, this death he brings. I say to you, he has already come among you in this world, this other King, of Death . . .

SOLDIERS. No . . . No . . .

JOHN. I say to you: that King who has come down into this world till now, he is that King of Death. He has already walked among you: here: pretending love but bringing Death. He is already turning you to stone. Listen.

SOLDIERS. No . . . No . . .

CHUCK. No Sir . . . No Sir . . . We should know him . . .

JOHN. How should you know him?

CHUCK. He would – be . . . ug-ly . . .

JOHN. If he came to you ugly, how should he have you love him? Must not this Death come down among you with a smiling face? Hiding, beneath this smiling face?

They look at him, bewildered.

I do not hide my face. (*He removes the mask.*)

SOLDIERS. He is . . . He is – like us . . . Only . . . only more – ea-sy . . .

JOHN (*removing crown, robe, etc.*). Help me . . .

BLACKIE (*suddenly*). Soldiers; help the King.

They do so, wondering, awed. JOHN *stands among them, man.*

CHUCK. We were certain till now. We knew everything a soldier should know. Now suddenly everything is – broken . . .

They look to JOHN.

JOHN. Oh soldiers. A text you ask of me, older than all speech. A picture must I bring now: image, like a dream, to trouble you: to beat its wings within these heads, within each head, and trouble it and have you wake and have you rise and in your rising haul your brothers with you, up, up, up, up into the light of the Sun.

There was a soldier once. He worked in a palace of stone. And all the rooms were stone, and all the walls were stone. And one day as he worked, suddenly before him the great rock opened wide, and he saw before him there the Light of Paradise; and beneath that Light of Paradise, the eternal sea. Many waters. And high, above those many waters, there came, on its milk white wings, like a milk white angel, a milk white creature of the air. So beautiful, a white sea bird. The soldier had never seen such a thing as this, in all his days: strange, high above the many waters, the cold cold waters, the milk white bird of the sea: coming: and with such song: to him, the soldier. He was afraid. The great white bird of the waters — frightened him. Such fear he felt. He ran. He ran through all the palace, stone door behind him, stone wall behind him, stone wall behind him. But ever, always in each room with him, the milk white bird, the beating of her wings above his head; and the song she sang. For him had she come; and he was in such terror. Wild, dreading, with his poor fists in their gloves of gold he struck out at the bird, lashed beat and struck. I cannot tell you the terror that he felt; but you can make it in your heads, the terror that he felt. For he thought she would destroy him, make him — not be. He fought, he fought: the wild black terror in him took him over absolutely.

The bird lay: fallen; her white wing, broken; a crimson wound in her white breast. She would never rise in the air again. And up within the soldier came a sadness: a desolation: that he had done such a cruel thing, of which there could be no undoing. The milk white bird was dead. He shook his head: 'No, no,' he said, 'I have done wrong. I do not know why, but something tells me this is — like a — sin that I have done. Oh come to me again, beautiful white bird of the many waters: I am so sorry, I could not help it: come to me again, I shall not fight you next time . . . ' But he knew. The milk white bird of the sea comes only once for a man. Once only for a poor benighted soldier. He tried to stand. He was so heavy. The gold that had been his glory weighed him. He was stone.

Silence. Soon we are hearing that distant ghost of the chasmstroke again. All in-self drained:

Tell the others this.

BLACKIE. The King is sad.

JOHN. Ay. All the pictures in my head are gone. Down, into — these heads . . . And they must work here.

CHUCK. You shall come to us again?

JOHN. Oh yes. To spend what little last of me is left, to drive yous all before me, up, into the light.

CHUCK (*daring barely breathe the name*). Paradise . . . ?

JOHN. Into your proper Kingdom. But I tell you: this other King, of Death, shall also come: pretending love, but angry in his heart, to turn you all to stone. And here's how you shall know him. By his robe. From neck to hem, his King's robe shall be torn. You tell the others this!

His task is done; there is nothing he can do but go. The SOLDIERS *stand amazed — their vision has departed. Suddenly:*

BLACKIE. We must hide this.

They stow HOLST's *body into the rock.*

CHUCK. He said, tell the others.

Night still. Gentle seasound. JOHN *bringing armful of regalia emerging spent from cave,* YESCANAB *following.*

YESCANAB. Well John.

JOHN. Well Stephen.

YESCANAB (*pause*). Me to the ship then. And not to loss me road this second time.

JOHN. Ye never lost it the first time. Ye found it. What'll ye do?

YESCANAB. No doubt it'll be some — delinquency, in the cities of the world. The landfall's likely to be Glasgow. Well. Thank your father. And you. I burn a candle in my head. For your — ministry. And everything.

JOHN (*pause*). Look after yourself.

Suddenly YESCANAB *is touching him; then gone.* JOHN *stands, astonished at the gift. Then:*

On.

Rends the robe with a grim vehemence from nape to hem, and goes.

From the dark sea-comb now lifts itself, to flail the desolate waste, seething and scything the conjured wind, an elemental thing: devouring, giddy, wild. Stormbeach, in night-darkness, lashed: the ocean and the rock in trouble. Wind a scourging fiend. CHILD MANATOND.

CHILD MANATOND. Break. Break. Head. Brea-eak. Sheela out. Brea-ea . . . Brea-ea . . . (*Striking, jabbing skull in vain.*)

Stone head Sheela. Hea-vy. Grave stone head stone hea-vy, off of me, up Sheela, split head, break — Break. Head. Sheela break! (*Clawing, pounding skull: in vain. Wind scourges on.*)

Ay. Head is tomb, tomb is empty, none here, Not's house is this. Huff, wind, puff, blow ma house down, Sheela to stand. Ffff. Ffff. (*Blows, screams like the wind, smashing her skull upon the rock:*) Break! Break! (*In vain.*)

Break!! (*In vain.*)

Wind is curling away, tumult abating.

Wind didny see me. Wind luiked thrui me. No me to see. Hi, Not. Poor Not poor Not poor Nobody poor None poor Not, how's all of Not the-day? What day? What's 'day'? The Sun is black.

Looking up madly as to it. Cold deadly light; a figure coming. But in CHILD MANATOND *some new prehension.*

This is not Not. If I is not . . . then who is I, to not be . . . ?

It is SISTER CROY *come: something terrible to tell. Not knowing what to call* CHILD MANATOND; *whether even to touch her. Beyond, the* MEN *of the islandhood are slowly laboriously coming, mouths masked, hands and forearms smutted:* YAGG, ELDER YESCANAB, *some burden between them, wrapped in a sail.* NEAND, *grave.*

Ha ha. An funerell. Whui's this when it's at home?

SISTER CROY. Puir Sister Duinhead. Her stormlamp. Set her

house ablaze. But for thon wind it hadny happened. Scourged her house clean. Made like a beacon of it.

NEAND. Devourin' flame.

SISTER CROY. Not one possession.

Exhausted, choking, islandmen have to set their burden down. CHILD MANATOND — *they would resist, but allow her this perhaps they must — opens the sail.*

CHILD MANATOND. Oh . . . Duinhead, Deadhead . . . Ug-ly . . . An taste o' the Lord's Wrath, was He sweet? (*Closes the sail.*) Guid . . .

Goes from them — and from SISTER CROY's *tentative reaching — on brink of some inner disturbing. Islandhood continue away, bereft and strangely centreless.*

Cold day, leaden. Silence. But for all-but-inaudible chasmstroke, a mere tremor afar below. MISS WEMWOOD. NEBEWOHL *surveying through fieldglasses.*

MISS WEMWOOD. The days are turning very short now, Doctor.

NEBEWOHL (*abstracted*). Yes. — Strange. Miss Wemwood, have ever you noticed that white rock before?

MISS WEMWOOD. Should I?

NEBEWOHL. This is Old Sandstone: all this coast is black. That stack is white.

MISS WEMWOOD. Someone must have painted it white.

NEBEWOHL *has focussed and seen; is offering her the glasses to see for herself.*

Those things give me vertigo.

NEBEWOHL. The rock's alive. Good God. Alive with them.

MISS WEMWOOD. With what?

NEBEWOHL. Gannet. What a bird. There must be thousands there. They weren't here yesterday . . . Strange: what group-organic reflex is it, what mechanism of choice, by which these so suddenly . . . arrive . . .

Silence.

MISS WEMWOOD (*suddenly*). Doctor.

When she has his attention she has him listen.

NEBEWOHL. The heartbeat of the Pit has stopped.

It has. Suddenly they are hurrying away.

Act Five

Midwinter dusk. Thin wind, voicelike afar, semitonally down-plaining.

BENGRY. Christmas Eve, and childrenless. Barely two in the afternoon, and all but dark. This deadest hour. Will nothing move? a wren? a crow? (*Listens.*) Christmas is a time of children, where are mine . . . ? Is times I think I hear them. (*Listens; wind fades to silence afar.*) Christmas, all but sonless: one living frozen tongue of flame alone, to lighten all this — desolation.

Slow creak of wheelchair laboriously approaching: MANATOND.

MANATOND. Pastor? (*No response.*) A've brought ye an gift. Sir. Painted, mine self; and come, mine lone, till offer ye. (*Silence from BENGRY.*) Pastor. Take. (BENGRY *takes.*) Open. See. (BENGRY *carefully unwraps; sees. Says nothing. In* MANATOND *a strange urgency somehow.*) Rachel, weeping. For her children, that they are no more. Herod has slain . . .

BENGRY. Thank you. Brother. Manatond.

MANATOND. I — I'm sorry Pastor. What an stony home to you our island have been. And crueller, to yuir princes of sons. Devouring them . . .

That wind briefly heard spare above the wastes afar.

BENGRY. Why Brother: I rejoice. If Death devour them, as you say. A seed will split a rock. Also I have still one son, haven't I? To feed this Death?

MANATOND. Pastor? Pastor, not this bitter scourging heart, A beg ye: with us. Gentle with our island. We do not always know what it is we do. F- forgive us . . . ? L-ove yuir enemy?

BENGRY. My enemy is no man. Brother. Only this Death. Our only love for him must be in our destroying him; no? But Death himself: think, Brother: what's Death's love for a man? But to come for him, to take him and to leave him ruin in his arms? Poor Death, wouldn't you say? For that to be the only love he knows?

Silence, wind fallen. MANATOND *cannot meet* BENGRY's *eyes, yet cannot escape them.*

An' I met this Death, I would not be gentle with him.

Soft, cloaked, terrible afar, the foghorn sounds. Tearing himself from those eyes, MANATOND is painfully wheeling himself away. Gloom thickens, BENGRY watching him.

Yes Brother. It is time.

Foghorn afar, somewhat clearer.

Last son of light, go down upon your journey now.

Darkness, fog. Foghorn nearer, its long C-note swelling, falling at last to its soft executional A-stroke. MANATOND in the wheelchair, writhing spasm-seized: struggling, not to stand, rather to staunch some motor-compulsion in him hauling him, neck upwards to his feet.

MANATOND. No . . . No. . . Leave me . . . (*Before our eyes two beings struggle for possession in him: the gentle cripple pleading; the monstrous king erectile, racking him.*) — Never . . . — I was asleep . . . So rested . . . Leave me in peace . . . — I wake . . . — No . . . (*Foghorn, hard, compelling, seems to have MANATOND all but rise.*) No . . . !

JOHN (*bringing CHILD MANATOND, blank*). Child Manatond. Your father.

MANATOND. Down . . . Down . . . Up. Up.

CHILD MANATOND. Da . . . ? Father . . . ?

MANATOND. Away you. Out, out, out . . .

CHILD MANATOND. Poor father, no, A help ye . . .

MANATOND. Hands off of me! Filth-thing! Ugh. Ugh. (*Some pathic loathing.*) Who is this? Down. Up. King. Royal. Rise. (*Half-risen, he spills forward, the chair falling.*)

CHILD MANATOND (*screams for him*). Father!

MANATOND. Daughter . . . ? Sheela . . . ? (*Pleadingly seizes her hands. But foghorn shears in, vast, compelling, ugly, to wrest him from her, willynilly kinging him.*) Up. Up King. Break Manatond, King out! (*Staggering half-stood, beastlike.*)

CHILD MANATOND (*her voice beginning to fail her*). Ma'n father . . . have his leigs . . . ?

MANATOND (*blind, feral, drawn as though by scent alone*).
Where is mine robe . . . Royal . . . robe . . . (*Clumsily clawing,
soon bringing assuaging regalia from their hiding place.*)
Kingly: to stand . . . (*Clutching the robe around him.*) Haha
ha, the King is hatched!

CHILD MANATOND. FogKing . . . walks . . .

MANATOND. A . . . ? Tore . . . ? Rent? Robe? Raint? Yoke till
hem? (*In a wild beastgrief reels hissing, all but felled again.
Again the foghorn stays his lapse.*) Duty. The King must go.
It is the King's the King.

CHILD MANATOND. Oh father no —

MANATOND (*sniffing*). Ugh. Ugh. Wipe. Wipe. Wipe. Wipe . . .
(*But his wiping gestures are his donning, first of crown, then
of mask. He steps backwards from her like some titan automaton.*)

CHILD MANATOND. A duina see it. A dreims it . . .

JOHN (*soft*). Ye see it. Sheila.

CHILD MANATOND. Father! Look at me!

KING. Filth off of me. No filth out of me! Wipe! Off. Wipe. Wipe.
Clean. All stone below, head only is a mahn. Head. Up. Proud.
Upright. Head's a mahn. I am the King of Heads.

CHILD MANATOND. Father, look at me.

KING (*sees nothing where she is; nor smells nothing now*).
Nothing . . . (*Seems puzzled.*) Nothing is here. Down, King.
Among mine clean sons.

Foghorn, easier. KING *staggering away.*

CHILD MANATOND (*nightmare-dumb yet manages to thrust
voice after him in some supreme self-obliterating effort*).
K — ill him . . . ! K-ill mine father . . . ! (*Reeling.*) No . . .
No . . .

JOHN (*staying her fall*). Yes. Yes Child Manatond. Yes.

CHILD MANATOND. No . . .

JOHN. Yes. Yes Sheila Manatond. Ye know it. You know it.

CHILD MANATOND. I want to sleep. Down. Down. Intill the
deep deep dark.

JOHN. You sleep then. Gently. Sleep the dark night away. Down . . .

CHILD MANATOND. John hold Sheila. Brother John not let go Sister Sheila's hand.

JOHN. Ay. Brother John come down with sister Sheila in the dark. Sheila wake alone . . . Your head this road. This way the morning comes.

Silence.

BENGRY (*quiet there*). John?

JOHN *can neither move nor speak.*

What are you looking at, John, so sad?

JOHN. The world.

BENGRY (*a moment; then:*) Well. You have seen it.

JOHN *is riven as at last to rail at him; instead, going only. Explosions from that distance in the earth.*

I remember. When John was very young. How much he wanted a little sister. Oh he would pester, cling, clamour: 'Get me a sister Da, a little sister to play with in our garden.' 'Oh' I would say 'sisters don't come for asking only. They have to be made.' 'Of what?' 'Of dust.' 'How does this dust become a sister?' 'Why, when there breathes into the dust the spirit of life.' Found him one day. In our garden; kneeling. Before him a little heap of dust and clay and leaves, all shapen clumsy like a — child. 'Tell me, Father. What must I do now, to have breathe into this the spirit of life: and make a sister?'

He is going.

Seismic tremor soft below. Explosion, sharp. NEBEWOHL hurrying with documents along gallery above; tremor continuing, progressively nearing.

NEBEWOHL (*selecting papers etc:*) Burn . . . Burn . . . Ministry . . . Burn . . .

Minor explosions, here, there, nearer; a ripping of rock. Approaching like some gathering eruption far below, inchoative tumult of some ascending human multitude.

JOHN (*his voice only, heard through several speakers, from that deep distance, railing*): Up! Up! Into your proper Kingdom, who you are! Shine like the Sun! Your light has come!

NEBEWOHL. Who is this man?

Explosions; tremor nearer.

Burn . . . Burn . . .

MULTITUDE. UP! UP! UP!

MISS WEMWOOD comes hurrying in for more documents to burn.

MISS WEMWOOD. Still they are coming. It's like some monstrous eruption. So many. I'd no idea such a number —

Hurries laden off. Metallic explosion, sharp, near.

NEBEWOHL. How did this start? Where from this first spark of disaffection in their stupid minds? What was the original seed of this?

MISS WEMWOOD (*hurrying back for more*). Not that all are abreacting. You can console yourself your discovery is not totally disproved. Some are fighting their way down! Down, Doctor, of their own accord!

NEBEWOHL. Stop blathering Wemwood. Our plane is waiting. Bring these.

Explosion dangerously close: tremor growing, to shake the theatre now; human tumult like a tornado upcurling. NEBEWOHL takes one last look round.

Damn. Damn. Damn. All over again I must begin . . . (*Hurries off after.*)

JOHN (*his voice*). UP! UP! Up, all of you! Out, over the wall! Out, upon the earth! Let all the morning hear you! Cry to it: 'a-Alleluia!'

CHILD MANATOND is wakening. The tremor advances, a shattering vibrance. Shocksounds, rock-ruptures; fracture by fracture spreading, the schism and the rending of the rock itself. The tremor and the roar rise to a momentarily obliterating apex; bedded in this culminating stroke, the flashing shock of the snapping of some chthonic metal core. Inrush, colossal, of the deep itself; the rocks fall, monument- ally colliding and engulfed. CHILD MANATOND holds her head in agony and wonder. Slowly now, the seism and the inundation fade; a last isolated rending and collapse; somewhere, a swift upflaring rising major third on a trumpet; the seism throbs away; that trumpet flare, farther; the seism fades. Silence.

CHILD MANATOND. Hear them. Hear them . . . Pastor? Pastor
Bengry? Hear them. Hear them, your son has freed . . . Hear
them: pour upward, out, from the belly of the rock. Hear
them: run out upon the earth; hurl themselves upon the wall,
tear with their hands at the stone, all the length of the wall;
from end till end of it tear at the stone, tear out the stone,
tear down the stone, the wall till rubble, a tooth of it all that
is left . . . They clamber the heaps of the rocks; claw, howling
like wild things up the mountainside, tug up through the
tangle and thorn to the stone spine of it; run, shrieking down,
toward the houses and the sea . . . Some do not: but fall to
the earth, delve it wi' their hands. Some stand, stare upward
at the sky and stars. One weeps. One, slower nor the rest,
stumbles like he's never held his weight before: slow, slow:
finding his way . . . The Great King is dead. The Great King
is dead. Pastor . . . ? John your son has brought the tower of
death to dust. I come to thank you for him: and for his young
brothers too, who have been — more than sons . . .

Oh . . . Oh . . . What is this I am . . . ? Flesh? Hand? Breast?
Eye . . . ? Oh . . . What is this: cold at my feet . . . Cold.
Cold . . . yet where it touches, warming me? The great deep
. . . ? Waters . . . ? Wild, wild . . . yet such . . . still . . . deep in
them . . . ? Oh deep. Strange deep. Strange, lovely deep. Tender,
yet what wrath in your caress . . . Take me. Deep, make me
yours, then I am mine. Bring me from me, then I am. I give
you me, and I am given me.

Oh I was asleep. And dreamed. Three stars of light came down
a while, and danced among these stones. Oh, brightest and
best of all the morning's sons, was I asleep? and did yous
waken — me . . . ?

Appendix

Sister Duinhead's hymn in Act Four.

The words are by Charles Wesley, the tune my own:

The time-values must be observed strictly, but to fluid rather than rigid effect. Because the melody changes key, the resumption of its opening phrase for stanza 2 is tricky.

DR.